A CAPITAL FOR THE NATION

☆

STAN HOIG

Illustrated with photographs and old prints

COBBLEHILL BOOKS
Dutton   New York

ILLUSTRATION CREDITS

Federal Writer's Project, 4; *Frank Leslie's Illustrated Newspaper*, 68, 81, 83, 93;
Gleason's Pictorial Drawing Room Companion, 101; *Harper's Monthly*, 99; *Harper's
Pictorial History of the Great Rebellion*, 14; *History of the United States Capitol* by
Glenn Brown, 6, 23, 24; Stan Hoig, *ii*, 36, 54, 85, 107, 123, 125; *Illustrated London
News*, 49, 52; Library of Congress, *vii*, 12, 15, 19, 28, 32, 33, 34, 39, 43, 46, 65, 67, 71,
75, 79, 88, 91, 98, 103, 104, 115, 118, 119; The Mount Vernon Ladies' Association, 95;
Jimmie L. Rogers, 114, Western History Collections, University of Oklahoma Library, 57.

Library of Congress Cataloging-in-Publication Data
Hoig, Stan.
A capital for the nation / Stan Hoig.
p.   cm. Includes bibliographical references.
Summary: Examines the history of Washington, D.C., and how it was
built, with an emphasis on such historic buildings as the White
House, Capitol Building, and Washington Monument.
ISBN 0-525-65034-2
1. Washington (D.C.)—Juvenile literature.   2. United States—Capital
and capitol—Juvenile literature.   3. Washington (D.C.)—History—
Juvenile literature.   [1. Washington (D.C.)—History.]
I. Title. F194.3.H65 1990 975.3—dc20 90-2783 CIP AC

Published in the United States by Cobblehill Books,
an affiliate of Dutton Children's Books, a division
of Penguin Books USA Inc.
Published simultaneously in Canada by
Fitzhenry & Whiteside Limited, Toronto
Designed by Mina Greenstein
Printed in the U.S.A.
First Edition   10 9 8 7 6 5 4 3 2 1

To the memory of
PIERRE CHARLES L'ENFANT

Acknowledgments

There are a number of persons and organizations whom I wish to thank for their assistance in producing this book. Heading this list is my wife, Patricia C. Hoig, who shared my enthusiasm for this project and aided greatly in its preparation. Others include Senator David Boren and his staff assistant Amy Johnson, who arranged for tours of the Capitol and White House; and my good friend and literary adviser, Brent Ashabranner.

Contents

Foreword

☆ Each year millions of citizens come from every part of the nation to visit Washington, D.C. They are people of all races and persuasions: families, schoolchildren, college students, members of clubs and organizations, farmers, business people, politicians, vacationers—Americans all, who wish to see and experience the nation's capital.

In doing so, they inevitably touch the national past and with it the ideals of a great democracy. Washington is a city of edifices, memorials, statues, commemorative parks, and other heroic symbols. These address themselves to different people and events—but they all say "America, one nation indivisible . . ."

To view the capital without a sense of its history is much like watching *Oklahoma* or *South Pacific* without hearing the music. Certainly, there is great beauty to see and enjoy in our capital: the magnificent buildings, the grand statuary, the dancing fountains, the enthralling art, the spacious landscapes.

Little is more inspiring than to stand on the west portico of the Capitol and enjoy the sight of the Mall extending westward to where the Washington Monument sends the eye soaring skyward.

But there is so much more. In Washington one walks in the footsteps of famous countrymen whose thoughts and deeds helped establish the world's greatest democracy. Occasionally a visitor must wonder: What great men of the past—presidents, congressmen, jurists, generals, and other men and women of history—have stood at the very spot where I now stand? And can one not see there on the east steps of the Capitol the timeless parade of newly elected Presidents of the United States, raising their hands and swearing allegiance to the Constitution as multitudes of other Americans applaud?

Perhaps the visitor can visualize George Washington walking these grounds as he plans his great capital city, see the erect figure of Thomas Jefferson striding up a dirt path to be inaugurated at the unfinished Capitol building, witness Abraham Lincoln signing the Emancipation Proclamation, or hear the lingering echo of Daniel Webster's booming cry in the Senate chamber: "Liberty and Union, now and forever, one and inseparable!"

The issue of national identity is deeply embedded in the lore of our capital city. The threat of disunion hung over the head of President George Washington like Damocles' sword. It tested the character and courage of Abraham Lincoln, survived a bloody Civil War, and ultimately found resolution in the hearts of Americans who know intense pride as a people and a nation.

It is all there, the record and remembrance of America's rise to greatness and her struggle to maintain cohesion among a diverse and often differing citizenry. Washington, D.C., is in itself our most precious symbol of national being, a reminder to all of us of the historic roots of our republic and the democratic principles upon which our freedom as a people so depends.

A CAPITAL FOR THE NATION

Washington City has just begun to emerge from the bucolic landscape along the Potomac in this view from Georgetown.

L'Enfant's Dream:
The Capital City

———

I

☆ On the morning of June 28, 1791, President George Washington strolled southeastward from the small settlement of Georgetown, Maryland. He wished to reexamine the grounds of the newly created ten-mile-square Federal District, which Congress had authorized by acts in 1790 and 1791, and decide upon sites for the public buildings. With him were architect Pierre Charles L'Enfant and surveyor Andrew Ellicott. The three of them would search out the best locations for a Capitol building, the president's home, and attendant government buildings for the new capital city.

Washington was pleased that the three-man commission he had appointed to oversee the planning and building of the capital had chosen to place his name upon it: "City of Washington." They had also given the Federal District the title of "District of Columbia."

As he walked, Washington enjoyed the quiet countryside which rose and fell with green hills and valleys. The bucolic landscape was broken by rail fences, planted fields, and occasional farm homes. A feeling of excitement began to grow inside the tall, calm-natured Virginian. No one knew better than did he the historic significance of the moment.

A capital for the struggling republic—a great nation eventually, he prayed—was about to be created. On these wooded acres there would one day be a grand city of magnificent buildings and tree-lined boulevards. It would be a city upon which Americans of future years could look with pride as a symbol of their national unity.

This was very important to Washington. Still in his initial term as the first president, he harbored a deep concern that the new government, facing dissension and discordance from all quarters, would not survive. He fervently hoped that the establishment of a capital city would help unite the previously autonomous and fiercely independent states. With the recent admission of Vermont, there were now fourteen states. Soon there would be others. But it was not at all certain how long they would hold together as one nation.

The location of the capital was of vital concern. Southern states, fearing domination by the North, believed that a capital in their region would bring settlers and commerce. The issue was so vital to them that it threatened their continuation in the Union. Virginian Thomas Jefferson would later note that never in his day had the Union been so near to dissolution.

The crucial matter was resolved when Jefferson and New Yorker Alexander Hamilton worked out a compromise at a supper meeting. Hamilton agreed to support the placement of the capital in the South if Virginia would support the assumption of Revolutionary War debts by the federal government.

As a result, the Congress voted in 1790 to make Philadelphia the capital for the next ten years while a permanent location on the Potomac River was decided upon. Numerous towns and states began bidding for the prize. Each anticipated great benefits in wealth and prestige if it won out. The competition soon became intense and bitter.

With the particular site still unresolved, Virginia and Maryland together offered a ten-mile square (one hundred square miles split by the Potomac) to the government for the capital, plus money for federal buildings. The U.S. Congress accepted the proposals, leaving it up to President Washington to select the exact location along the Potomac.

Washington, whose home was at Mount Vernon just a few miles downriver, had chosen this site between Georgetown and Alexandria. He had long believed the Potomac River would become the main artery of commerce westward from the Atlantic. Anxious to get the project under way, Washington had reacted favorably to a letter from L'Enfant pleading that he be allowed to play a role in the creation of the national capital.

L'Enfant, a native Frenchman, had fought for America in its War of Independence. After the war he had settled in New York, where he worked as an architect and engineer. When he heard of the proposed new capital, he wrote to President Washington asking for the chance to share in creating a capital "magnificent enough to grace a great nation."

"No nation, perhaps," he noted, "had ever before the opportunity offered them of deliberately deciding on the spot where their capital should be fixed."

His vision of a grandiose capital city had appealed to Washington's appreciation for noble architecture and his belief in America's potential as a great nation. Though almost opposite in personality, the cool-minded, pragmatic Washington and temperamental, idealistic L'Enfant shared a common feel for grandeur in the creation of a national capital.

"A century hence," Washington wrote to a friend, "will produce a city, though not as large as London, yet of a magnitude inferior to few others in Europe."

So eager was L'Enfant to go to work on his masterpiece that he secured no contract from the government. Indeed, he was not even

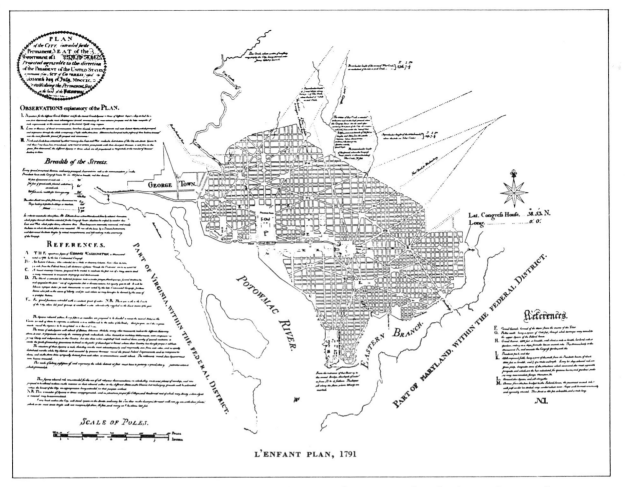

L'Enfant's original plan for the capital city provides the basic design of modern Washington, D.C.

officially hired. Having only Washington's verbal instructions to proceed with a plan, L'Enfant had plunged wholeheartedly into his work.

Now as the three men toured the Federal District, L'Enfant acted as guide. Using a partially completed map he had prepared from an earlier reconnaissance, he enthusiastically outlined the plans he had conceived for the city.

The gifted Frenchman called particular attention to a wooded prominence known as Jenkins Hill (now Capitol Hill), which lay just to the east at the bend of a marshy rivulet. It was the perfect place, he insisted, for the Capitol. Later, he would bestow upon this high point his famous description of it as a "pedestal waiting for a superstructure."

A hundred years earlier a planter had dubbed Jenkins Hill "Rome," as though it were prophetically foreseen as another Capitoline Hill crowned by the ancient Temple of Jupiter. He had also named the stream "Tiber Creek," after the famous Italian river overlooked by the city of Rome. Others knew it as "Goose Creek."

Stretching out from this elevated vantage point, L'Enfant visualized, would be broad, spacious avenues. They would extend in diagonal lines that intersected with others, producing an orderly grid pattern for public buildings, businesses, and homes. At points of advantage would be circles appropriate for statuary and fountains.

On a rise at the head of Tiber Creek northwest of Jenkins Hill stood an orchard. This was a spot that had caught Washington's eye from the first. It was an ideal site, the European architect agreed, for a presidential palace. As he listened to the Frenchman's glowing visions, Washington caught an imaginative glimpse of a city of the future. In his mind's eye he could see a resplendent executive mansion at the site of the orchard.

A towering Capitol building with a glittering dome would grace Jenkins Hill. Connecting it with the president's home would be a great ceremonial boulevard—as today's busy Pennsylvania Avenue so often becomes. And extending directly westward from the Capitol, L'Enfant told the president, would be a "vast esplanade," a broad Mall. It would contain an ideal location for an equestrian monument where the westward view from the Capitol intersected the southward view from the president's house.

Washington might well have visualized the Mall; but he could hardly have foreseen that one day at the end of that long esplanade

An early artist's drawing depicts L'Enfant's grand vision of broad Pennsylvania Avenue, linking the executive mansion with the Capitol, seen here in the distance.

a towering obelisk dedicated to his memory would strike magnificently against the western sky.

There were others who were equally optimistic regarding the Potomac site. John Vining, a legislator from Delaware, declared:

> I wish the seat of Government to be fixed there because I think the interest, the honor, and the Greatness of the country require it. I look on it as the centre from which those streams are to flow that are to animate and invigorate the body politic. From thence, it appears to me, the rays of Government will most naturally diverge to the extremities of the Union.

On April 15, 1791, surveyor Ellicott and a group of citizens from Alexandria fixed the first stone marking the southern corner of the ten-mile-square area at a site known as Jones' Point just south of the village.

"May the stone which we are about to place in the ground," toasted Alexandria's mayor, "remain an immovable monument of the wisdom and unanimity of North America."

The development of a national capital did not come easily for the struggling, impoverished democracy. The government had no money, and much was needed. Landowners along the Potomac were expecting to make large profits from the sale of their land. But during an earlier visit, Washington had shrewdly worked out a reasonable price from landholders in the Federal District by implying that the capital might still be located elsewhere.

The only way the government could raise needed funds was by auctioning off lots in the proposed capital city to the public. It was first necessary to produce a drawing of the city plan that could be engraved and printed. But the uncompromising L'Enfant dallied in producing the plat. He feared it would aid speculators in buying the best locations in his architectural vistas. They would build shanty houses, he thought, and ruin his creation. This delay seriously hampered the sale of lots.

Further, L'Enfant's broad streets of 100–110 feet wide, avenues 160 feet wide, and one grand avenue 400 feet wide infuriated the landowners. During negotiations, Washington had persuaded them to give up land for roads at no charge. Then, when one of the largest landowners erected a manor house in the new city, L'Enfant overstepped himself. He raged that the house damaged the aesthetics of his plan and had it demolished.

Reluctantly, Washington dismissed the Frenchman. When he departed, L'Enfant took his detailed city plan with him. Development of the city was turned over to Ellicott. He was fortunate that Benjamin Banneker, a brilliant, self-educated black man who had been on the Federal District surveying team, was able to reproduce L'Enfant's map from memory. Ellicott had the map engraved and it became the master plan for the city of Washington. L'Enfant was so disturbed by the omission of his name from the map that he refused to accept the offer of $2,500 and a lot near the president's house in compensation.

Funding problems, arguments between architects and builders, and lack of professional labor in the area stymied progress. Despite this, a slow beginning was made on the capital. The walls of the executive mansion and the north Senate wing began to rise. However, by 1800 the two structures were still far from being completed.

Congressman John Cotton Smith of Connecticut, arriving in late November of that year, penned a description of the new settlement. It presented a dismal scene. As his coach neared the location, Smith could see that one wing of the Capitol had been erected on Jenkins Hill. A mile distant, the white sandstone structure of the president's mansion stood out sharply against the disrupted, wintry landscape.

There were no recognizable streets except one rutted road with two buildings on each side of it—today's New Jersey Avenue. Pennsylvania Avenue did not exist, the whole distance from the Capitol to the president's house being a deep morass covered with alder bushes. Between the executive mansion and the small village of Georgetown stood six newly erected buildings. At other locations were scattered a dwelling house or two and a few wooden shacks. Most of the low area of the city was marshy and brushy. The paths in every direction were muddy and unimproved.

The story was told of an ardent young Frenchman who visited the city at this point in time. He had heard much of the new American capital and finally realized an opportunity to view it.

"*Mon dieu, quelle grande ville!*" he exclaimed fervently. "*Elle ne manque que de maisons et des habitants pour être la plus* *grande ville du monde!" "*My God, what a great city! It only wants houses and inhabitants to be the greatest city in the world!"

A census taken of Washington City (as it had become known popularly) at the end of 1800 showed a population of just over 3,000 people, including 623 slaves. Most of the elected officials and government employees depended upon nearby Georgetown and Alexandria for accommodations and domestic needs. However, new businesses and boardinghouses soon began to open in Washington City.

Still, the roads remained rough and rutted with potholes that were dangerous to after-dark traffic. Pedestrians were often plagued with either boot-deep mud or suffocating dust. Civil pleasures were few, though on November 24 the new Washington newspaper, the *National Intelligencer*, announced the first "dancing session" of the season.

During the early years, the federal government left civic improvements to the impoverished city, and beautification was slow to come. The U.S. Treasury finally approved President Thomas Jefferson's request for money to plant fast-growing Lombardy poplars along Pennsylvania Avenue.

Two two-story brick buildings were built near the president's home, one for the Treasury on the east and one to house the State and War departments on the west. A government Naval Yard and Arsenal were established south of the Capitol along the Eastern Branch, or Anacostia River. Streets were hacked out along surveyed routes, and builders began to scatter a few homes, tenement houses, and taverns over the still rustic landscape.

In 1803, Benjamin Latrobe, an architect who had migrated from England, received an appointment from Jefferson to redesign the Capitol building. Latrobe later designed a number of the city's outstanding structures, including St. John's Episcopal Church. He also played a key role in the Washington Canal project.

The canal, originally conceived by L'Enfant, ran eastward from

Tiber Creek near Seventeenth Street along the north side of the present Mall, veering south in front of the Capitol to the Anacostia River.

The War of 1812 with England was a severe blow to Washington City. In 1814, the British came to burn and pillage the American capital. The Capitol building, executive mansion, War and Treasury buildings, Naval Yard, Arsenal, and Potomac Bridge were all destroyed or badly damaged by fire.

A heavy rainstorm prevented much of the city from burning. An unusual tornado which struck the city killed several British soldiers, and still others died while blowing up the Arsenal. The disasters caused the English invaders to withdraw from Washington.

There now arose an outcry from some politicians to move the capital away from Washington. One opponent of the idea declared that if the capital were moved ". . . half of our patriotic pride and prestige as a people will be lost forever." A motion for removal was presented in the House of Representatives, but the idea was killed when the House voted 83 to 54 to remain in the District of Columbia.

In 1815, Latrobe was recalled to handle reconstruction. A housing boom flared in the area around the president's home, which by now had come to be known to many as "the White House." Several new churches were erected also, and stores sprang up along Pennsylvania Avenue. Bridges across the Potomac and Anacostia added to the traffic of people already arriving in the city by steamboat and stagecoach lines. Some streets were graveled, a few board sidewalks were laid, and a few scattered oil lamps were installed.

Architects George Hadfield and Robert Mills influenced the city's appearance with their building designs. These two men extended the classic Greek architecture in structures spread between the Capitol and White House.

But it was grandeur amid squalor. As the population of Washington climbed to about 15,000 during the 1820s, the city's problems of housing, water, sewage, and streets became more and more acute. The area fronting the view west from the Capitol, L'Enfant's esplanade, had become a swampy wasteland.

On July 4, 1828, ceremonies were held for the start of two important new projects. One marked the beginning of work on the Chesapeake and Ohio Canal from Georgetown, which connected with the old Washington Canal at Seventeenth and B Streets. The other was preparation for the projected arrival of the Baltimore and Ohio Railroad.

Trains began running from Baltimore to Washington in 1835. However, the city refused to permit locomotives to run inside the city limits until the B&O built its depot north of the Capitol in 1852. During that period, the cars carrying passengers and freight were horse-drawn from the city limits to sheds at Second and Pennsylvania. A much appreciated city improvement was the asphalt and gravel macadamizing (so-called for its Scot inventor John L. McAdam) of Pennsylvania Avenue.

But there were still serious deficiencies in the Washington landscape. Cows, swine, and poultry rummaged about freely in the discarded garbage of vacant lots. Neat neighborhoods of brick homes were separated by areas overgrown by weeds and strewn with rubbish. Streets still turned into quagmires when it rained.

Shanties, cheap saloons, and hostels filled the slum areas between the marble edifices of government. Alleyways had become the desperate homes for black freedmen and their families. Slave traders operated within the shadow of the Capitol.

An English writer who visited the city during this period wrote:

> Everybody knows that Washington has a Capitol, but the misfortune is that the Capitol wants a city. There it stands, reminding you of a general without an army, only surrounded and followed by a parcel of ragged little boys, for such is the appearance of the dirty, straggling, ill-built houses which lie at the foot of it.

However, some important developments took place during the decade. In 1844, the National Observatory was completed to the west of the White House on the bank of the Potomac. George Washington had once camped there with the forces of General Edward Braddock. In 1846, Congress, as requested, ceded back to Virginia its portion of the original ten-mile-square District of Columbia west of the Potomac. The first gaslight illumination was installed on the Capitol grounds and along Pennsylvania Avenue in 1847.

This artist's view of a neat and orderly Washington in 1852 adds the Capitol's new wings a decade early, but shows the old Bulfinch dome and Robert Mills's unused design of the Washington Monument.

By the end of the fifties, Washington's population had grown to over 40,000, far outstripping its neighboring cities of Alexandria and Georgetown. Though still with serious shortcomings, the city had made many improvements in its civic and social institutions. Of particular note was the red-sandstone Gothic castle of the Smithsonian Institution, erected between 1847 and 1855 facing L'Enfant's proposed Mall. Another addition was the Corcoran Gallery of Art, its French Renaissance structure destined to become a famous Washington landmark.

As the decade of the sixties began, with the outbreak of the Civil War, most improvements ceased. The war would add its own stark effects upon the landscape of the national capital. Military posts and encampments dotted the periphery of the town. Troops marched incessantly here and there. Herds of mules, horses, and cattle trampled through the streets while supply wagons and artillery clattered by night and day.

Barracks, stables, wagon sheds, warehouses, makeshift hospitals, and other military appurtenances all added to the chaos. These disruptions were joined by a flood of refugee black people from the Southern states seeking asylum in the District.

Many of the wartime changes were temporary; some were permanent. One remaining postwar affliction was "Murder Bay," a triangular area formed by Pennsylvania Avenue, the canal, and Fourteenth Street. It was notorious for its vice and criminal element. Another serious detriment was the infestation of huge rats which plagued the city. But with the war's end, the military tents disappeared, and gradually the city returned to civilian normalcy.

A new Capitol dome now towered above all other structures in the city. The introduction of a streetcar system brought the sight of horse-drawn trolleys moving about on tracks along the centers of Washington avenues. A significant alteration of city planning evolved during the postwar era when a large business community began to sprout up around the old Center Market

A balloon view of Washington in 1861 shows a domeless Capitol, an unfinished Washington Monument, and the Washington Canal cutting through the Mall.

that had long operated at the site of the present National Archives.

In 1866, the city government spent $75,000 in dredging muck from the canal and filling in the swampy area fronting the White House. The federal government refused to lend aid to such civic improvements. However, it abetted the Mall concept by aligning its new Agriculture building just to the west of the Smithsonian and fronting it with thirty-five acres of ornamental flowers and shrubs.

The grand design of L'Enfant was largely forgotten during the postwar development of Washington. One striking disruption of the plan had occurred in 1855 when tracks of the Baltimore and Ohio Railroad were laid across the Mall in front of the Capitol. Though an outcry was raised in Congress, the tracks lay rusting and untraveled until the Civil War, when the military made good use of them.

By 1871 the nation's capital had far outgrown its neighboring cities of Alexandria and Georgetown.

L'Enfant's dream was further aborted when a second railroad, the Baltimore and Potomac, was permitted to build its massive Gothic-style depot at Sixth and North B streets in front of the Capitol. Its train sheds extended almost the width of the Mall. Equally as intrusive was the grandiose "French Renaissance stone pile" of the State, Army, and Navy building (now the Executive Office building) erected between the White House and the Potomac.

In 1871, a Board of Public Works was created to oversee a program of civic improvement. A dominant figure on this board was Alexander R. Shepherd, whose aggressive leadership greatly improved the street and sewage systems. Pennsylvania Avenue was paved with wooden blocks and beautified.

The canal was dredged, replaced with an underground sewer, and filled in. Trees were planted, and dilapidated structures were torn down. Though Shepherd spent the District of Columbia into bankruptcy, he produced a city with expansive stretches of paved, well-lighted, tree-lined boulevards. These improvements were further enhanced by a wave of monuments to some of the great men of American history such as Andrew Jackson, Abraham Lincoln, and Ulysses S. Grant.

One of the most important actions taken in creating the modern city of Washington was the reclamation of the marshy land between the Washington Monument and the Potomac River known as the Potomac Flats. Dredging and filling of the area, periodically flooded by rises in the Potomac, began during the summer of 1882 and continued past the end of the century. Today this is the site of the Lincoln Memorial, the Jefferson Memorial, and the Vietnam Memorial.

In 1887, L'Enfant's original manuscript was rediscovered by city planners. However, this still did not prevent construction of the Post Office building at an off-angle to Pennsylvania at Twelfth Street or locating of the ornate Italian Renaissance building for the Library of Congress where it stands on Capitol Hill.

The McMillan Committee of the U.S. Senate began a study in 1901 that would ultimately encompass the design of the entire District of Columbia. In doing so, the committee again brought forth the documents of L'Enfant, using them to model an enlarged plan of a modern twentieth-century metropolis.

Thus at the end of one full century, the basic concepts of L'Enfant were deeply embedded in the structure of the nation's capital. More importantly, as L'Enfant had visualized and George Washington had so fervently wished, the city had truly become an august setting for the Capitol of American government, the president's home, and other emblems of national unification.

L'Enfant was ill-rewarded for his contribution. Penniless in later life, he could be seen with a cane shuffling along the streets of Washington, his long, green coat buttoned to his throat. In one hand were clutched papers which he hoped would cause Congress to award him the $95,500 he was asking for his services to the country. Moody and lonely, his only apparent friend was the little dog that followed him about.

Though Congress finally awarded him about $3,800, L'Enfant died broken in spirit in 1825. He was buried in a pauper's grave in Maryland. In 1909, a repentant Congress had his body disinterred and laid in state in the Capitol Rotunda—one of the twenty-seven men (including Unknown Soldiers of four wars) ever so honored. He was reburied at Arlington National Cemetery, where a monument was erected in his memory. His greatest tribute, however, is the capital city which will forever bear his imprint.

The Capitol Building

2

⭐ The creation of a capital city had not come easily for the new American republic. Nor would the completion of its house of government—the Capitol of the United States. It would take thirty-one difficult years from the time the cornerstone was laid by George Washington before the twin houses of the legislature were finally joined into a single edifice, five more before the plan of the original building was deemed to be completed.

A feeling of joy and festivity had reigned on that day of September 18, 1793, when President Washington arrived to dedicate the Capitol. After boating across the Potomac from Alexandria, the tall Virginian first marched his way to where the initial excavations were being made for the new president's home. Trailing him was the entourage of officials, citizens, uniformed artillerymen, and formally dressed Freemasons walking two-abreast "in the greatest solemn dignity, with music playing, drums beating, colours flying and spectators rejoicing."

After pausing there to visualize a palatial mansion standing majestically above the Potomac, the procession moved on. Now the parade became irregular as Washington led the way through the swampy Goose Creek basin along the course of present Pennsylvania Avenue. Crossing the boggy stream by tiptoeing on stones and hopping from log to log, the group made its way up Jenkins Hill. There in a cleared spot a scaffold and hoist had been erected, and the historic cornerstone lay waiting.

Following Masonic rituals, President George Washington laid the cornerstone of the Capitol building.

As President of the United States, and also Acting Grand Master of Maryland's Masonic lodge, an honorary title bestowed for the special occasion, Washington played the leading role. The granite block was hoisted into place as the first president took up a silver trowel and a marble-headed gavel. The gavel had been especially for him to use on this occasion. With these instruments, he enacted the ceremony of laying the cornerstone of the original north wing of the national Capitol.

Washington placed on the stone a silver plaque which made record of the auspicious occasion. A prayer was said, the Masonic honors were chanted, and a fifteen-volley salute was fired by the artillery. The ceremony concluded, Washington and the others retired to a nearby booth where they feasted upon a barbecued 500-pound ox and other delicacies.

Washington would again view the still uncompleted Capitol wing in 1797 when, after ending his eight-year term as the nation's first president, he stopped by on his way from Philadelphia to his home at Mount Vernon. Both the Capitol and the president's home were yet under construction, as they would be when he died at Mount Vernon on December 14, 1799.

A design for the Capitol building had been selected in a government-sponsored contest which offered the winner a prize of $500 and a city lot. The competition was won by William Thornton, a Philadelphia doctor with no architectural experience, with his design of a colonnaded and domed center structure with two wings. Each wing would house a branch of Congress. Thornton's plan was lauded by Washington for its "Grandeur, Simplicity and Convenience . . . so well combined." Thomas Jefferson was pleased, too, saying that it "captivated the eyes and judgment of all."

The Treasury had only enough funds at first to commence the north wing, which would be forced to serve needs other than just that of the Senate. Constructed of sandstone from a Virginia quarry, the wing was near enough to completion by May of 1800 that the government began moving its records and paraphernalia from Philadelphia to occupy the building.

On November 22, President John Adams, wearing a formal coat, silver-buckled knee breeches, and powdered wig in the style of the day, rode up Pennsylvania Avenue, its ill-defined course blanketed with three inches of snow. In addressing the Sixth Congress of the United States, Adams congratulated the nation at large on its achievement in creating a capital city. Here, he prayed, the great virtues of its namesake, George Washington, could "be forever held in veneration."

About town the families of legislators and other government people had begun crowding into the limited and inadequate boardinghouses along New Jersey Avenue. Many congressmen were so distraught with their poor lodgings, crowded conditions, and rural environment of early Washington that they talked much of returning to Philadelphia. It was a subject that had long stirred the passions of politicians and would not soon go away.

Living conditions in the foundling settlement, so recently hewed from the rural countryside of the Potomac, were poor indeed compared to Philadelphia or many other locations. Whether or not it would long remain the capital city depended almost wholly upon the completion of a meetinghouse for the Congress.

It was difficult for the impoverished and badly indebted nation to make much progress on the building. The sale of lots, upon which the financing of public buildings depended, was slow and produced little revenue. There was a severe scarcity of professional masons, mechanics, and other workmen as well as building materials and equipment in the area.

With only the north wing for the Senate being completed, the House of Representatives met at first in the wing's west side. The building was also shared by the Supreme Court, the Circuit Court, and the Library of Congress. In 1801, the House moved to the site of a one-story, oval-shaped structure, known disrespectfully as the

"Oven." When the building was torn down in 1804, the House returned to its original meeting site in the north wing with the Senate.

An important new figure became involved in the creation of the Capitol in 1803 when President Jefferson appointed Benjamin Henry Latrobe as its architect. Born in England and educated in Germany, Latrobe came to America in 1796 and quickly won attention for his design of the Bank of Philadelphia and other public buildings. Under his direction, the House chamber was near enough to completion in 1807 that the representatives could occupy it, though it was not really completed until 1811.

Latrobe also installed a floor dividing the Senate chamber, with its high ceiling, into two levels. When this renovation was completed and leaks and cracks in the building were mended, the Senate occupied the new top floor. The Supreme Court held its sessions on the ground floor. Still, the two wings stood apart atop Jenkins Hill as separate structures amid a clutter of stonework and building materials, void of landscaping and without a unifying rotunda and dome.

When British troops under Rear Admiral Sir George Cockburn entered Washington City late on the evening of August 24, 1814, the two congressional meeting halls were connected only by a temporary passageway and an unfinished semicircle wall of red brick that had been raised as part of the Capitol rotunda. Cockburn, the story goes, perched himself on the chair of the Speaker of the House and challenged his men to burn "this harbor of Yankee democracy."

Tossing chairs, desks, papers, books from the Congressional Library, and paintings, including the portraits of Louis XVI and Marie Antoinette which had hung in the Senate chamber, into piles and adding tar barrels as tinder, the British set both wings ablaze. The conflagration spread throughout the two buildings, gutting them, destroying their roofs and blackening their walls with fire and smoke.

By good fortune, a rainstorm struck that night and put out the smoldering fires. But when morning came, the Capitol of the United States stood as two empty shells, with ugly black smudges marking the white sandstone exteriors above each window. The British had written taunting slanders and drawn disparaging cartoons on the ruined walls of the Capitol.

Indignant Americans accused the British of barbarous behavior in sacking and burning the Capitol. There also arose a loud clamor from politicians to remove the national capital to another site. The suggestion was vigorously attacked by editors Joseph Gales and William Seaton of the *National Intelligencer*. The editors saw the Capitol ruins as "elegant skeletons" of national pride. The paper passionately challenged those who would move the capital away from Washington, asking: "Do the smoky walls and ruins of conflagration strike terror into the hearts of the beholders?"

Prior to the British attack of 1814, a covered walkway connected the House and Senate chambers.

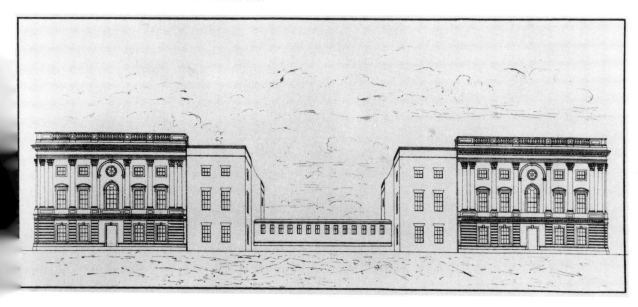

The Capitol building stood as an "elegant skeleton of national pride" after its burning by the British in 1814.

"What!" one fervent patriot reportedly exclaimed. "Desert the Capitol? Let Congress rather cover it with canvass and sit in its ruins than abandon it at this moment!"

The impracticability of this action, however, became apparent when a soldier climbed atop the Capitol ruins and began walking adventurously around the parapet rim. The wall gave in, and the man fell to his death.

Arrangements were made to house the Congress in what had once been Blodget's Hotel (at the northwest corner of Seventh and E streets). It had recently been used to house the General Post Office and Patent Office. Early in September, the building was inspected and approved by President James Monroe for use by the Congress. The legislative routine of business was continued immediately, along with much wrangling over whether or not to move the capital.

To counter the possibility of losing the capital, local citizens formed the Washington Building Company. The group raised money to build a temporary home for the Congress. By May of 1815 a substantial brick structure had been erected on the site of the present U.S. Supreme Court building. Here, in what became known as the "Brick Capitol," the Congress met for the next four years, thus preserving Washington, D.C., as the seat of empire for the nation.

During 1815, Congress authorized $500,000 to rebuild the Capitol buildings, and President James Madison appointed three commissioners to superintend the project. Latrobe was recalled to head the restoration. Working with a group of Italian designers, the architect set about to redesign the two wings, make the House chamber into a semicircular shape and add twenty-two round and two square marble columns. The Senate chamber would also be enlarged and redecorated.

On July 4, 1816, citizens meeting at McKeown's Hotel toasted the anticipated revival of the Capitol . . . "Its domes, its sanctuaries, and its temples . . . rising in strength and beauty above the reach of ruffian torches."

However, the work went slowly, and the Capitol was still a "congregation of rubbish, of new materials, of unfinished and dilapidated walls." It was also the butt of much jesting when President Monroe took office in the spring of 1817. He responded by declaring that Americans saw "the smoke high curling to the shaded skies" as a challenge to their national pride and expressed his hope to have the Capitol restored and completed by the end of his term.

This work was still far from finished when the talented Latrobe resigned in 1817 in a dispute with his governmental superiors. He was replaced by Boston architect Charles Bulfinch. The two charred wings still stood forlorn atop Jenkins Hill, looking as if they had been ripped apart by a giant hand and abandoned. The Senate chamber featured a low dome; the House had none.

They continued to draw much scorn and ridicule. The *National Intelligencer* angrily expressed its wish that it would soon see the day when "fops and witlings dare no longer spend their senseless jests on the Capitol of the United States."

The goal of uniting the two units into one with a "Centre Building"—the rotunda and dome—was a principal objective of planners. Finally, on August 24, 1818, the cornerstone for the domed rotunda was laid in a simple ceremony conducted by the Commissioner of Public Buildings. As refreshments were served to the project workmen, it was publicly noted that the date was the anniversary "of the day the barbarous enemy made war upon the arts, upon literature, and upon civilization."

By August, 1819, its foundations and subterranean vaults were nearly completed. The western wall had been bricked two stories high, though the eastern or front wall was still only a few feet above ground.

Top priority was being given to readying the halls of Congress for use. Great blocks of Virginia freestone and variegated marble, some weighing as much as five tons, were floated down from quarries forty miles above on the Potomac. The blocks, used to create the twenty-two columns for inside the House chamber, were unloaded from the Washington Canal near the Capitol. They were then hoisted aboard especially stout wagons and hauled up the hill. There stonemasons went to work at shaping them into the giant pillars.

On July 4, 1819, citizens of the town gathered at the Washington Tavern on Pennsylvania Avenue and marched in a procession to the hall of the House of Representatives. At noon the Declaration of Independence was read. As the building neared completion that fall, the *Intelligencer* provided its readers with a description of the remodeled House of Representatives.

The chamber had been changed to a semicircle, its inner circumference lined with twenty-two large columns of variegated breccia or Potomac marble. The multicolored pillars were topped by scrolled capitals made from Italian white Carrara marble.

Above the canopy-covered speaker's dais perched a large American eagle, and towering above it, a heroic-sized statue of *Liberty*. Her right hand holds the Constitution of the United States. To her left, the serpent of wisdom entwines around the base of the column. The figure is now on the south wall of the chamber, which today is known as Statuary Hall.

Over the entrance door, a toga-draped, allegorical figure in marble represents *Clio*, the Muse of History, by Carlo Franzoni. Riding in the winged chariot of *Time*, she records the proceedings of the nation as she passes over a celestial globe on which the signs of the zodiac are carved in relief. A wheel of the chariot is a clock.

A bas-relief of *Fame* and a profile bust of George Washington once adorned the room. The domed ceiling was decorated by Italian Pietro Bonani (or Bonanni) with a design similar to the dome in the Roman Pantheon. From high in the center of the dome hangs a retractable giant chandelier, now converted from candle to electric light.

A painting of the House of Representatives was done by Samuel F. B. Morse—the same Samuel Morse who later turned to scientific experiments with the telegraph and invented the Morse code.

While the chamber was pleasing to the eye, it was deadly to the ear. Sound reverberated so harshly that speakers could rarely be heard. In an effort to improve the acoustics, crimson drapes were festooned behind the pillars and the furniture was reupholstered. These efforts failed to improve the situation, as did draping the walls and carpeting the gallery. A glass frame was installed below the dome. A failure, it was removed.

The suggestion that the speaker's chair be placed in front of

"Who can look upon the building without feeling his bosom swell with pride?" asked a writer when the east portico and steps were finally added.

the room entrance and new doors opened on either side of it was ignored. Instead, a wooden partition was erected in the rear of the colonnades, but it was taken down after a few weeks.

On December 6, 1819, five years after the British attack, the U.S. Congress reoccupied its Capitol. Still, what Washingtonians saw against the eastern skyline were the two wings connected by a domeless center wall. Work on the center building continued slowly.

By November, 1820, the internal walls of the rotunda and a

portion of the roof had been raised, along with the west external wall. The wooden frame of the dome was in place two years later when a capital visitor climbed atop it for a "picturesque and sublime" view of the city.

On December 9, 1822, Bulfinch reported that the western projection of the building had been completed by copper-sheathing that side of the dome, painting the walls, inserting window frames and sashes, and removing the scaffolding. Iron railings between the columns of the loggia were yet to be installed. Work was under way to cover the remainder of the dome and crown it with a railed skylight, twenty-four feet in diameter, that helped light the rotunda below.

Bulfinch carried through with much of the original plans of Thornton and Latrobe, installing the connecting rotunda and the stately columned east and west porticos and steps. However, he is best remembered for his copper dome which added a vital unifying classical element to the appearance of the Capitol. He also added smaller domes with cupolas over the two wings at this time.

By the summer of 1823, the *Intelligencer* could proudly announce that from its windows could be seen the "magnificent Capitol rearing its copper-sheathed dome among the clouds." It was another year before the interior of the rotunda was finished. Though the east and west porticos yet remained to be done before the building would be completed, the two wings of the Capitol of the United States of America at long last stood as one structure.

The rotunda was opened to a gala reception in October, 1824. In attendance were the Marquis de Lafayette—the French aristocrat who had served General Washington so courageously and well during the Revolution—and a huge crowd of government officials, Washingtonians, and others.

Most paintings and published views of the Capitol as it was at this time fail to show the numerous chimney stacks that marred the beauty of its roof line or the brick foundation work which was visible before the east and west porticos and steps were added. These last were still under construction in 1826.

On the east, the twenty-four columns that today grace the Capitol front, were being hewn from giant blocks of Potomac freestone, some 240 feet long and three feet in diameter. Workers were also busy on the triangular pediments roofing the porticos, building the steps, and leveling the land in front. Calls were made to beautify the "sacred" grounds and make them the "grand and principal promenade of this, the Capitol of our Union."

In the fall of 1828, the scaffolding and work sheds were removed from the east front. Now it was possible to fully appreciate the artistry of Luigi Persico, a native of Naples who created a bas-relief design for the triangular tympanum over the east front entrance.

The central and principal figure in the classic design depicts the spirit of *America*. At her feet is an American eagle, representing the bird of Jove, or Jupiter—who in Roman mythology rules over all other gods and people. On her left is the figure of *Hope* who directs the attention of *Genius*, the guardian spirit of people at birth, to the bright prospects open to her. On her right, *Justice* indicates the righteous restraint which a pure morality has created to regulate the conduct of men and nations.

Inside the building were now displayed four large patriotic paintings by artist John Trumbull, who had been commissioned by President Monroe to produce them for the Capitol. The assigned subjects were *The Declaration of Independence, The Surrender of Cornwallis, The Surrender of Burgoyne,* and *Washington Resigning His Commisson.*

For several years after the paintings were completed, they were hung in small rooms of the Capitol with poor lighting. Finally, in 1826, they were moved to the rotunda of the Capitol, where it was originally intended they be placed.

During 1828, improvements were made in both the House and Senate. The hallway leading to the House chamber, once narrow and dark, was enlarged. In the Senate, the vice president's chair, which had been relocated, was returned to its former position. Member seats were arranged in a semicircle facing it.

Also, improvements were made in the Senate gallery for the convenience of the public by removing an unused upper gallery along with the columns that supported it. This made the room airier and permitted a flood of light to enter from a row of windows which had been mostly concealed.

A new door was added to the west front of the building, and the embankments there were smoothed and planted with grass. The outside walks were widened, graveled, and lined with silver fir, linden, and elm trees. On the outside of a brick wall surrounding the building, a belt of native trees and shrubs was planted.

"The Capitol at Washington is finished," a visiting scribe announced in June, 1829. He praised the building as a truly magnificent structure and spoke effusively of its view at sunset "from the noble terrace on the west side." A Washington journalist joined in with a proud claim that: "No one can stroll along the terrace on the West front of the Capitol, without admitting that it is one of the most beautiful promenades in this country."

A writer for the *National Intelligencer* was similarly taken with the beauty of the Capitol and the view it presented:

> . . . how delightful it is in the cool of the morning or evening to ascend the Capitol Hill and there take a view of the picturesque scene which surrounds the City of Washington . . .
>
> On the summit of the hill, commanding a view of this delightful scene, and the City of Washington, stands the Capitol—a fit emblem of the Republic, grand, beautiful, and irregularly great; the Temple of Freedom and Law. Who can look upon the building without feeling his bosom swell with pride?

Completion of the edifice with its great, impressive rotunda and lofty, hemispherical dome signified a regal crowning of a na-

The Capitol grounds were fenced and landscaped by 1848, though the area beyond was still dirt streets and a rural setting.

tional capital. Though to many Americans it was a hopeful symbol of unity for the nation, political harmony remained tenuous at best during the years that followed. It was largely in the Congress where the vital issues of state were fought as the new republic struggled to find its course into the future. Looming above the deliberations of Congress was the great contention that existed between Northern and Southern states—the foreboding issue of slavery.

Here, in the halls of Congress, great men such as Henry Clay of Kentucky, John C. Calhoun of South Carolina, and Daniel Webster of Massachusetts occasionally rose above the usual tedious oratory and petty bickering to speak with eloquence and force on matters that troubled the nation's soul.

In the meantime, the country was expanding farther and farther across the vast empire of western America, bringing more and more senators and representatives to the Capitol. Additional space was needed to house the deliberative body, and in 1850, Congress approved money for the extensions to both wings of the Capitol.

The Civil War was still in progress when the new dome and two new wings were completed in 1863.

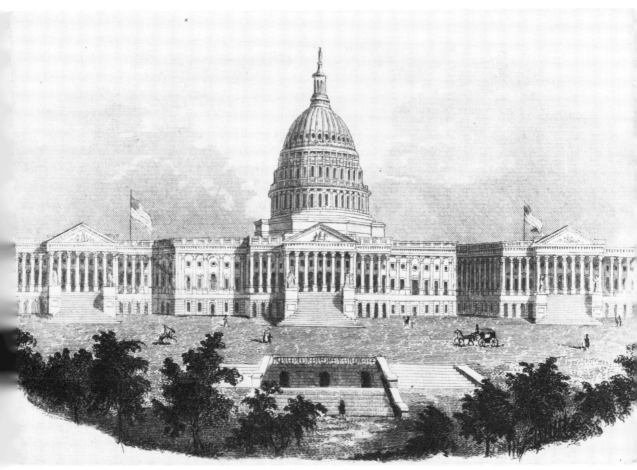

President Abraham Lincoln joined a large crowd as the bronze statue of Freedom *(originally called* America*) was hoisted atop the new Capitol dome on December 2, 1863.*

With President Millard Fillmore presiding, the cornerstone for these was laid on July 4, 1851, amid the firing of artillery and the ringing of church bells.

Daniel Webster delivered the oration, giving blessing to the success of the Union and its Constitution. But for all of Webster's heartfelt thanks, during the following decade it was to be that as the Capitol grew, the Union continued to dissolve. The bitter friction between abolitionist and proslavery elements grew more and more passionate. More and more, Southern leaders talked of secession.

In December, 1857, the House moved into its yet unfinished wing; the Senate followed suit in occupying its new chamber in January, 1859. Both bodies brought with them such intense factionalism and rancor that they would soon prove the wisdom of words spoken by the man who was elected president in the fall of 1860—"A house divided against itself cannot stand."

When the Southern states began seceding early in 1861, the Capitol stood as a shattered symbol. The old low Bulfinch dome, badly in need of repairs, had been taken down. It was being replaced with a much taller, more impressive cast-iron dome designed by Thomas U. Walter.

Scaffolding and scattered stonework scarred the beauty of the Capitol and its grounds. As the little-known President-elect Abraham Lincoln arrived in March to take his oath of office, many doubted that he had the strength to hold the republic together. There was good reason to wonder if enlargement of the Capitol had not now become a futile endeavor.

On December 2, 1863, a large crowd gathered on the Capitol grounds to witness the hoisting of the statue of *Freedom* to the cupola of the new dome. Originally the 19-foot statue had been designed to wear a "liberty cap," the symbol of a liberated slave. However, on the orders of former Secretary of War Jefferson Davis, a crested warrior's helmet had been substituted.

The bloody Civil War was ended in 1865; the Union had survived. By 1867, virtually all of the new addition and remodeling of the Capitol had been completed. Nearly a century later, in 1961, the Sam Rayburn extension of the east front central area added beauty and needed working space to the Capitol.

Today, Americans can gaze with immense pride upon their magnificent Capitol building. Unquestionably, it would have pleased George Washington greatly.

The Capitol building in Washington, D.C., today.

The White House

3

☆   The presidency shared a level of power and importance with the Congress in the new republic. But in a symbolic sense, it was supreme. The office had been established with great reluctance by the framers of the Constitution. They feared they might well create another authoritarian power such as that of King George III of England, under whom they had suffered. Yet, at the same time, many Americans yearned for a dignity of state equal to that of European aristocracy. The president would be the prime representative of national prestige, and his home the American edifice to rival European palaces.

The concept of a "presidential palace" had been fostered by L'Enfant, whose European mind saw the American capital in regal terms. The idea was not unappealing to Washington. His life-style at Mount Vernon had been much in the vogue of a country squire. Although Washington had known the hardships and rigors of field and forest, he held an appreciation for gracious living, fine clothes, and palatial architecture.

Washington and the Federalists were already under criticism

for being too monarchial. Because of this, they were careful to avoid language that gave support to the charge. "National" was seldom used, and they preferred to call the executive mansion "the president's house." It would be referred to by this name for some time before the title of "White House," which was known to have been used as early as 1809, became common. It is not known if "White House" was derived from its white freestone construction or from having been painted white as it is today.

An early-day artist presented a romantic setting for the president's house.

In March, 1792, open competition to find a design for the president's house was announced. The contest was won by James Hoban, an Irish architect who had come to the United States after the Revolution. His submission was a dignified but simplistic three-story structure similar to many European mansions of the day. Its north front was faced with four Ionic columns, a classic triangular tympanum over the entrance.

On the south was a circular portico with six columns. This entrance led inside to a large, oval-shaped drawing room. The building's hipped roof was trimmed with a Georgian-style balustraded railing. A large room across the east end, similar to one in Washington's home at Mount Vernon, would serve for state functions and receiving guests.

One of the features of the design which Washington and his selection committee liked most was its capacity for expansion. This could be done through the addition of wings at either end. The fact that Hoban was available to personally supervise the construction was also appreciated. He was awarded a $500 gold medal and a plot of land in Washington City.

Work on the mansion commenced immediately. On October 13, 1792, a party of Freemasons, the Federal District commissioners, and others paraded to the site from Georgetown to lay the cornerstone. The foundation had been completed, and the stone made ready at the southeast corner. After the dedication ceremony was performed, a polished brass plate inscribed with a record of the event was pressed into a base of fresh mortar atop the stone.

Washington was in Philadelphia and could not attend the ceremony. A year later when he arrived to lay the cornerstone for the Capitol, the basement walls stood thirteen feet high in the scooped-out hillside. When he again viewed the building in 1797, the stone upper-story walls stood with empty holes for windows and doors. They were crowned by the skeleton framework for the roof.

A crowd had gathered to see the retiring president, some standing on the mansion walls to do so. An artillery company which had been organized by builder Hoban fired a sixteen-gun salute. Then Washington went on his way. It is the last time he was known to have seen the White House.

Funding was as much a problem for the president's house as it was for the Capitol. Financial pressures caused not only delays in construction but, at the commission's request, the elimination of the top floor from Hoban's original design. The building was still not finished when Washington died in 1799. Even when John and Abigail Adams arrived the next year to become the first occupants, the interior was far from finished. The condition of her new home brought a discouraged comment from Abigail:

> Not one room or chamber is finished of the whole. It is habitable by fires in every part, thirteen of which we are obliged to keep daily, or sleep in wet and damp places. To assist us in this great castle, and render less attendance necessary, bells are wholly wanting . . . and promises are all you can obtain. This is so great an inconvenience that I know not what to do!

Far from being the palatial mansion L'Enfant had envisioned, the house was without lamps, mirrors, and many conveniences which the Adamses had enjoyed in Philadelphia and elsewhere. They were also forced to hire their own servants. The grounds were cluttered with work shacks and scattered stacks of stone, brick, and lumber. There being no place in the yard to hang her laundry, Abigail dried her wash in the large, unplastered, empty East Room—destined to become an elegant reception hall for visitors.

Congress had appropriated $25,000 for furnishing the house. With it, six rooms were made comfortable. Abigail began conducting weekly receptions, or levees, for government officials and dignitaries of foreign countries. John Adams, in his black velvet knee breeches and powdered wig, received the guests with a stiff, courtly bow. Adams' term of government court was short-lived, however, for his bid for a second term was defeated after only four months in the executive mansion.

Yet John Adams did leave behind a worthy contribution to White House lore. After spending his first night as the first occupant of the new president's home, he wrote a letter in which he said: "I Pray Heaven to Bestow the Best of Blessings on THIS HOUSE and on All that shall hereafter Inhabit it. May none but Honest and Wise men ever rule under this Roof!"

Today, these words are carved into the mantle of the fireplace of the State Dining Room as the White House prayer.

Adams was followed by Thomas Jefferson, who brought with him an air of indifference to formality. He and his Anti-Federalists had seen their victory as a virtual revolution over what they considered to be the Federalist aristocracy. Accordingly, he dispensed with some of the trappings of the White House inherited from Adams.

The coaches, horses, and silver-mounted harnesses were disposed of. He abolished the levees, but invited guests into the mansion on New Year's and the Fourth of July. Jefferson did not bow; he shook hands. Instead of buckled knee breeches, he wore trousers. His manner was courteous and informal but affable. To avoid the pomposity of rank, he installed a round dining table.

Still, Jefferson held a definite appreciation for elegance. Ever intellectually curious and inventive, he added his personal touches to the mansion. With the help of Benjamin Latrobe, he installed dumbwaiters, landscaped the grounds, planted elms and magnolias, enclosed the south yard with a stone fence, and built extensions on both ends of the house to serve as stables and storage rooms. Two earth mounds, still present, were created on the south lawn to provide visual barriers for privacy.

Jefferson made many changes to the interior of the mansion. Among the first was to install two water closets, or indoor toilets, upstairs and have the unsightly privy that sat beside the great house

Citizens and visiting dignitaries alike could enjoy an evening's stroll on the south ground of the White House.

removed. Further, he enriched the appearance of the walls, doors, and mantles with garlands, wreaths, and other decorative embellishments. The oval entrance room on the south become a drawing room. It was furnished in part with blue upholstery, giving it today's name of the Blue Room.

Being a widower, Jefferson utilized the services of the wife of James Madison, his secretary of state. Dolley (or Dolly) Madison, vivacious, fashionable and outgoing, was an excellent hostess. The buxom charmer undertook the task with a social grace befitting the president's home.

After two terms in office, Jefferson was replaced in the presidency by James Madison. Now mistress of the executive mansion in her own right, Dolley embellished her social activity with state dinners and receptions for congressmen and diplomats. She was popular with both men and other women. During her long tenure in what now was commonly known as the White House, Dolley brought personal charm, social grace, and elegance to the nation's first domicile.

She also introduced lavishness, excesses in gowns, shoes, and jewelry, and drove about in an expensive chariot. She used rouge, wore turbans, and dipped snuff. For this she had her critics, who felt that the White House was coming to resemble a bit too much the foppery of European capitals.

It all came to an end in 1814 when the British under Admiral Sir George Cockburn landed near Bladensburg and swept the American militia away to advance on Washington. President Madison had gone forth to observe the battle, and Dolley watched anxiously through her spyglass from the roof of the White House for his return. Finally, however, she was forced to flee, leaving behind a dinner table set with food and wine. In leaving, Dolley managed to rescue the White House silver, china, cabinet papers, and a portrait of George Washington.

The British actions in sacking and burning the capital could hardly have worse insulted American dignity. The Redcoats burned and virtually destroyed the White House along with other national buildings. While there, Cockburn and his men ate the food from Dolley's table and made vulgar toasts to "Jemmy's health."

The British piled furniture in the center of the drawing room and set it afire. When they departed, they left behind a gutted, roofless shell. The ruined White House stood as a stark reminder of the British humiliation of American pride and their contempt for the Union created by their one-time rabble colonies.

American officials moved quickly to restore the White House. James Hoban was hired to rebuild it. He found that many of the original walls had to be torn down, and the structure was virtually built anew. It took two years before the mansion was in shape for President James Monroe and his wife to move into it in the fall of 1817.

Those attending the public reception at the White House on New Year's Day, 1818, were far more representative of American democracy than those of James and Dolley Madison's day. There were men in boots and spurs, some smoking cigars and others chewing cuds of tobacco. Powdered wigs were matched by unruly heads that combs had seldom touched.

Aristocratic Elizabeth Monroe soon created an air of snobbishness by greeting guests from a raised platform and refusing to return calls made to the White House. Still, the well-educated Monroe, who had served as U.S. minister in France and England, brought to the White House a courtly dignity that helped restore American self-esteem.

The south portico was completed in 1824 under the direction of Benjamin Latrobe, its round facade, Ionic columns, and circular stairway giving the building a more stately appearance.

During John Quincy Adams' reign from 1825 to 1829, the White House returned to the stiff, unsocial days of his president father. It was a period of neither nobility nor commonality. Adams enjoyed morning swims in the Potomac, horticulture, and astronomy. He contributed to the White House appearance by having the grounds filled and graded and by personally planting and cultivating numerous trees. An American elm planted by Adams in 1826 stands today on the south lawn as the oldest tree on the grounds.

His wife, Louisa, hosted weekly receptions and met guests graciously. But John Quincy was disinterested in small talk and could

The rounded portico and curved steps of the White House's south front, designed by architect Benjamin Latrobe, were completed in 1824.

converse well only on subjects of his private interests. His distance from the common man may well have contributed to the White House's social revolution under the administration of Andrew Jackson.

One of the more memorable events of White House history is the public reception held by Jackson after his election. After the Tennessean had been sworn in by Chief Justice John Marshall on the east portico of the Capitol, the large crowd of well-wishers scurried moblike up Pennsylvania to the White House. Once there, they brawled, broke china, and tromped on the damask-covered chairs and sofas. Jackson found himself entrapped by the press of the crowd but finally escaped through a back door.

The White House under Jackson was open and friendly. Having arrived in Washington deeply in despair over the recent death of his wife, Jackson turned to the wife of his private secretary for his official hostess. Emily Donelson was not yet twenty-one at the time, but she soon proved herself more than capable in managing the White House social affairs. Through her management, the atmosphere was cheerful and relaxed but tasteful.

During Jackson's eight-year tenure, the north portico, which had been designed originally by Latrobe in 1807, was constructed. The tympanum, supported by ten heroic columns, was extended out from the building, giving that view a much improved majestic look. Formal gardens were created on both the north and south sides. An appropriation by Congress permitted the remodeling and refurbishing of the East Room.

Jackson's two-term administration ended much on the same unhappy note it had begun. Political difficulties, the tuberculosis death of Emily, and his own failing health left Jackson in a state of despondency. Further, his final public reception produced another fiasco similar to his first. A 1,400-pound cheese, presented to Jackson by New York citizens, had been put out for the occasion. The attending throng of rowdy visitors proceeded to smear the sticky cheese throughout the White House.

Martin Van Buren, who followed Jackson to the presidency in 1837, reacted to this intrusion of "mobocracy" by stationing police at the doors. Van Buren drove about in a grand coach and lived in luxurious style. Angelica Singleton, his daughter-in-law who acted as White House hostess, flaunted her aristocratic taste in long velvet gowns, feathered headdresses, and the formal announcing of guests.

In reaction to what he considered gross excesses, Representative Charles Ogle of Pennsylvania issued a lengthy oration flaying Van Buren and his lofty life-style. In essence, it was an attack against the concept of an American royal palace. To Ogle, the White House had become "as splendid as that of Caesar and as richly adorned as the proudest Asiatic mansion."

The Ogle "golden spoon" speech aided the old soldier William Henry Harrison in winning the presidency in 1841. When Harrison died of pneumonia only a month after his inauguration, his successor, John Tyler, returned the White House to a less affected social mode. The death of Tyler's invalid wife, Letitia, the next year further diminished social activities.

During his last year as president, Tyler was remarried to twenty-four-year-old Julia Gardner. The lovely and vivacious First Lady brought a brief period of gaiety to the mansion with dressy receptions and the sounds of laughter and waltz music.

The White House had now begun to serve as a national symbol in a significant new way. Delegations of American Indians from the far western frontier were being brought to Washington to visit the White Father. Government officials wished to persuade the tribes to accept U.S. autonomy and take up the ways of the white man. They hoped that visiting the capital and touring the White House would impress the Indians with the majesty of the United States.

Many such delegations of American Indians were brought to Washington, D.C., and the White House. One such arrived during the summer of 1846, following the Treaty of Comanche Peak in Texas. The delegation of Plains Indians and frontiersmen was escorted to the White House to meet President James Polk. Among them were the Comanche war chief Santa Anna and interpreter Jesse Chisholm, for whom the famous Chisholm Cattle Trail would later be named.

The long-haired president received the group upstairs in the Ladies Parlour. The Indians, who had been dressed in the white man's clothing for the occasion, were delighted at seeing themselves in the full-length White House mirrors. When they were escorted to the south grounds where the Marine Band was playing,

President James Buchanan is shown receiving an Indian delegation in the East Room of the White House.

the Indians quickly began shedding their uncomfortable shoes.

Performances by the Marine Band on the White House lawn had now become a regular twice-weekly event. Washingtonians came there informally on summer evenings to stroll about and, perhaps, even meet the president or Mrs. Polk. This democratic habit continued under the former general Zachary Taylor, who attended the lawn events ready to shake hands with anyone. However, most of the time his sickly wife, Margaret, remained secluded on the second floor of the White House and received only her closest friends.

When Millard Fillmore occupied the White House following Taylor's death in office in 1850, the New Englander held morning public receptions. His wife, Abigail, coming from an impoverished background, had been ill-prepared to handle the societal functions of the White House. Social affairs also suffered under Jane Pierce, wife of President Franklin Pierce. Grief-stricken by the death of their only son, she remained withdrawn from Washington society and public involvement. Visitors found the White House cold and cheerless.

When bachelor James Buchanan arrived at the White House in 1857, the hostess role was filled by his attractive, tactful, and poised niece, Harriet Lane. By virtue of her efforts and personal charm, state elegance was returned to the White House with official dinners and receptions. Buchanan, too, was a polished diplomat, being generally regarded as a brilliant host. During his administration, two significant social events took place: a reception for the first emissaries from Japan and a state dinner for the Prince of Wales, who later became King Edward VII.

Entertaining the British royal monarch was testimony to the rising stature of the American presidency in world opinion. By now the White House had clearly become an important emblem of American democracy and unity. But history would soon contradict that. A powerful issue that had long held Northern and Southern states apart was about to erupt into bloody war. Slavery!

The framers of the Constitution had not been able to resolve this monstrous problem. Now it had begun to threaten the very essence of national unity. As the threat of secession and the passions of war grew, a serious geographical fact was realized. The United States capital and the White House stood squarely between the two slaveholding states of Virginia and Maryland.

During the preceding years, Congress had refused to appropriate money for the mansion's upkeep. Its white walls had become tarnished. The majestic pillars were splattered with tobacco juice. Inside, the drapery had become tattered, the carpets badly worn. The decaying condition of the White House reflected the deterioration of the Union.

Several Southern states had already seceded when Abraham Lincoln arrived to assume the presidency in the spring of 1861. To many Americans, the White House which he and his wife occupied no longer represented a nation unified. History can record no time when the burdens faced by a president were greater than those which Lincoln knew during his stay in the White House.

Despite the mounting troubles of the day, the first levee of the Lincoln White House was upbeat. Though many Southerners stayed away, a huge crowd was in attendance as the lanky, somber-faced backwoodsman from Illinois greeted his guests. The genteel urbanite and political sophisticate mingled with the buckskin-clad Westerner and the artless agrarian. Scattered through the crowd was the gold of epaulets against the blue of uniform.

But the joyous receptions were short-lived. Quickly enough war came, bringing with it the sobering reality of death and defeat. Death, when a young man whom Lincoln had known well died in battle and his funeral held at the White House. Defeat, when the Union army was routed just across the Potomac at Bull Run in July, 1861.

Mobs of office seekers, contractors, and others asking for pardons or promotions for family members besieged the White House. Secretary of State William Seward complained that they filled the grounds, stairways, halls, and even the closets. Lincoln commented that he felt like a man who was letting rooms at one end of his house while the other was afire.

Mary Lincoln attempted to restore the lost beauty of the White House. Using the $20,000 appropriated by Congress for the purpose,

President and Mrs. Lincoln welcomed a variety of Americans to the White House on New Year's Day, 1861.

she redecorated the building throughout. Only Lincoln's office was exempted. A large reception was held on February 5, 1862, to celebrate the achievement. Though greatly admired by many, the beautification was criticized by some as being lavish waste in time of war.

Few had realized that on the night of the reception, the Lincolns' twelve-year-old son, Willie, was seriously ill. On February 20, 1862, the boy died, their second such loss. Both parents were plunged into the depths of gloom. Mary was too grieved even to attend the funeral. For some time after, Lincoln would shut himself alone in his room and weep for Willie. The White House was placed in mourning; all receptions were cancelled, never to be resumed during the Lincoln presidency.

Gradually, the news on the battlefront began to improve. This was followed by Lincoln's reelection as president and a huge victory reception at the White House. Then, at long last, came the great moment of joy when General Robert E. Lee surrendered to General Ulysses S. Grant at Appomattox. Once again, the White House stood for one nation.

Crowds of jubilant people swarmed up Pennsylvania Avenue and onto the grounds of the executive mansion. Bands played and celebrants whooped. It seemed almost as though the great storm of pain and suffering was over. But then came the morbid days of Lincoln's assassination and funeral. Again the White House was engulfed in a pall of despair.

Even when Andrew Johnson became the new tenant, the bitter factionalism and rancor of reconstruction divided the country and its capital. The Tennessean and his family were unpretentious, family people. There were always children and grandchildren about. First Lady Eliza Johnson was in such poor health that she let her eldest daughter, Martha, handle her official duties.

Johnson resided in the White House besieged by enemies. Only after he had escaped impeachment by a single vote did any sort of social buoyancy begin to return. Martha, wife of a Tennessee senator, was a practical, efficient woman—even to the point of keeping two cows on the White House grounds to provide fresh milk and butter. Martha also supervised a thorough remodeling of the White House.

On the night that Johnson was acquitted of his impeachment charges, a grand celebration was held at the White House. During the last year of his administration, extravagant levees were conducted, with the general public invited. But it was the adminis-

tration of Ulysses S. Grant which returned the pomp and glitter to the White House. Now attending its dinners and fêtes were titled figures from abroad as well as the new business, manufacturing, and banking rich of America. The gilded age had begun.

Gradually, bit by bit, the country began to find reconciliation. The wounds of war slowly healed. But, most importantly, the great issue that had divided the nation, slavery, was ended. Other difficult social and political problems would arise, but none of them would so threaten the unity of the nation or the White House as an eminent symbol of the Union.

Over the years many improvements and modifications have been made to the White House. Renovations were made to the East Room and the State Dining Room, and the main floor and stairway were reconstructed in 1902. The roof was replaced with steel trusses, and a fire-resistive third floor installed in 1927. But it was under the administration of Harry S Truman that the greatest improvements were made.

Between 1949 and 1952, the stately building was virtually gutted. Bulldozers dug a new two-story basement, and the structure was rebuilt on new foundations. One of the most apparent alterations was the addition of the Truman balcony at the second-story level of the south portico. Each succeeding presidential family has contributed to the refurbishing and decoration of the executive mansion in line with its historic character.

Today, through the stately beauty, magnificent art, and eloquent artifacts of history, the White House truly expresses the ultimate achievements of a great, unified nation.

When the north front of the White House was being renovated recently, smoke stains from its torching in 1814 could still be seen.

The Inaugural Ceremony

4

☆ Along with its capital city and attendant edifices, it was necessary for the new nation to develop its ceremonies of state. Unquestionably, one of the most significant was that of the presidential inauguration. Over the years, the affair has developed into a principal American event.

There is good reason. The inauguration ceremony serves to ennoble the presidency, the American form of government, and the nation itself. Further, it symbolizes the peaceful transfer of political power within the republic and provides a new beginning for the country. And, significantly, the inaugural helps ease the bitter rancor of political campaigns.

No precise form had been established for the oath-taking when George Washington arrived in New York City, then the nation's capital, a week before his scheduled inauguration as the nation's first president on April 30, 1789. Still, he was received in grand fashion by a welcoming committee of dignitaries, artillery salutes, brass bands, and swarms of onlookers who lined the shore of the Hudson River as he crossed from New Jersey.

The ceremonies began at about six o'clock on inauguration morning with the salute of artillery. This was followed by the pealing of church bells. Even as they sounded, the overcast sky which had been threatening rain suddenly cleared, delighting all. At noon military companies began gathering at Franklin Square, where Washington had taken residence with a friend. There were two mounted troops, a company of grenadiers, and a company of Scottish Highlanders in their colorful kilts.

President George Washington took his first oath of office at Federal Hall in New York City on April 30, 1789.

In the wake of swirling bagpipe airs and trailed by an entourage of dignitaries, Washington, dressed plainly in brown, rode in his carriage to Federal Hall. The building was old and rickety. Though repairs had been made, many were still fearful of it. Washington was met at the door by Vice President John Adams, who escorted him to the open balcony at the front of the building.

When the oath of office was read by the chancellor of New York, Washington responded with an untypical display of emotion. He reached down and took the Bible from its crimson cushion, kissed it, and with his eyes closed repeated the oath, adding: "I swear," and "so help me God!"

This done, the chancellor turned to the crowd and shouted: "Long live George Washington, President of the United States of America!"

The crowd responded with a roar of huzzahs and waving of their hats. After making a brief speech to the Congress, the new president was escorted to St. Paul's Church for a religious service, and then to his quarters. That night New York City was illuminated with brilliant displays. Particularly striking were those of the French and Spanish ministries. The streets were so crowded when Washington went downtown to see the sights, he was forced to walk.

An inaugural ball was held on the night of May 7 at the Assembly Rooms on Broadway. The president, who liked to dance, performed minuets and cotillions with various ladies. The ball was a societal affair with many prominent and wealthy people attending. A great deal of dazzling jewelry was worn by the women. Additionally, each of them carried a fan on which there was a medallion bearing the likeness of Washington.

The first inauguration had no sooner concluded than a chorus of complaints was heard from the Anti-Federalists, who thought that the affair had been much too imperial. The cry of "Long live George Washington!" they said, was much too akin to tribute paid the British monarch with "Long live the King!"

Thomas Jefferson, who was much opposed to public show for

the inauguration, was at the lead of this opposition. At the start of Washington's second term in 1793, both Secretary of State Jefferson and Secretary of the Treasury Alexander Hamilton encouraged the president to hold a private ceremony without display or even an inaugural speech.

Further, some newspapers were beginning to denounce the president for having monarchial tendencies. Washington was criticized for his lavish, cream-colored French coach, ornamented with cupids and flowers, and for joining the Philadelphia aristocracy in a social life distinguished for its gaiety and glitter.

Washington overruled his secretaries and held the ceremony in the Senate chamber before both legislative bodies at Philadelphia, which had become the capital city in 1790. He also made a short speech. Overall, the second inauguration on March 4—the day set for presidential inaugurations—was a quiet, modest affair. Still, it was noted by some that its audience was not the general public but the wealthy people of society.

In 1797, John Adams succeeded Washington as the second president of the United States. The event was significant in that it set a pattern of peaceful change of administration that has been a hallmark of American government. Further, it marked the retirement of the nation's most beloved figure, George Washington. New Englander Adams was filled with a sense of history. He realized that the idea of the "sun setting full-orbed, and another rising, though less splendid . . ." was a unique experience for the new republic.

The idea of taking part in such a public exhibition made the unpretentious Adams extremely nervous. Nonetheless, he concurred with the Federalist concept of the ceremony as a valuable symbol of state. His many years of service in the royal courts of Europe had instilled in him a liking for their grandeur. Determined to play his role as well as he could, he purchased a new carriage that was "simple but elegant enough" and uniforms for his coachman and footman.

He wore a knee-length suit of gray broadcloth, and at his side dangled a handsome sword. The weapon seemed somehow out of character for the rotund Adams. Another affectation was a cockaded hat which, because of the powdered wig on his head, he carried under his arm.

Adams' entrance to the chamber of the House of Representatives in Philadelphia was made easier by the firm, towering presence of Washington at his side. The great emotion which Adams felt in taking the oath was matched by that of the crowd. Undoubtedly it was the departure of Washington from public office that brought tears and choking throats to the audience. But the inaugural address delivered by Adams was stirring, also.

He spoke eloquently of America's resolve in winning independence and praised its good sense in adopting the Constitution. Free and honest elections, he reminded the audience, were the underpinning of the republic. And he implored his countrymen to support the development of public education as the only means of protecting a democratic government from its natural enemies.

The speech was received with rousing applause. He was later visited in his quarters by Washington, to whom he had paid great tribute for his wise administration of government. Washington congratulated the new president and wished him good fortune.

There had been great harmony in Adams' succession of Washington, with both political and personal accord between the two men. But when Adams departed the presidency, it was much different. Embittered at not being reelected, he was at severe enmity with Jefferson, whom he personally blamed for his defeat. Adams refused even to attend Jefferson's inauguration. On its eve, March 3, 1801, he worked late in the White House. Then early the next morning, Adams left the city in his coach.

The inauguration of Thomas Jefferson was the first to be held in the new capital of Washington. The Republicans had publicly scoffed at Adams' "coach-and-six" and his attempts to imitate the lavish ceremonials of European courts. Jefferson wanted his inaugural to set a less pretentious, more democratic tone for the presidency and government.

The citizens of Washington, nonetheless, were in a mood of celebration for the event. They were joined by a large number of visitors from outlying areas who had arrived in town for the event. Soon after the Washington artillery company sounded its guns over the city, the streets became filled with people. At midmorning the artillerymen and an Alexandria company of riflemen paraded in front of Jefferson's lodging place at Conrad and McMunn's tavern two blocks from the Capitol.

At noon Jefferson was met at his door by a party of citizens and congressmen. He was plainly dressed, and there was no coach awaiting him. Without fanfare, but trailed by his escort, Jefferson made his way on foot to the Capitol. Upon his entry into the chamber of the Senate, the only wing of the Capitol then standing, the artillerymen fired a salute.

The congressmen all rose as Jefferson entered the chamber. Vice President Aaron Burr, who had lost the presidency by the most narrow of margins, vacated his presiding chair in Jefferson's favor. Though he had once tried to dissuade Washington from inaugural oratory, Jefferson chose to address the Congress with a short speech. Making note that it was the majority which ruled in a republic, he stressed another principle of democratic government.

". . . that though the will of the majority is in all cases to prevail, that will, to be rightful, must be reasonable; that the minority possess their equal rights, which equal law must protect, and to violate would be oppression."

After finishing his address, Jefferson approached the clerk's table and took the oath of office administered by the Chief Justice of the Supreme Court. That done, Jefferson was escorted back to his lodging by the chief justice, the vice president, and others. Though Washington citizens celebrated that night, there was no parade nor inaugural ball. The third president of the United States was perfectly content to remain in his lodgings and rub shoulders with his fellow boarders for another two weeks while the White House was being prepared for him.

On his second inauguration in 1805, Jefferson again spoke to the two houses of Congress in the Senate chamber, this time *after* taking the oath of office. Though there was no official or prearranged celebration, Jefferson was met by a large concourse of lawmakers and citizens outside the chamber. They were joined by an impromptu procession of workers from the Naval Yard who carried banners displaying their various trades. Marching to military music, they escorted Jefferson up Pennsylvania Avenue to the White House.

This obvious desire of the common citizen to celebrate the presidential inauguration defied the Jeffersonian desire to subdue the ceremony. When Jefferson left office in 1809, those restraints were forgotten. James Madison was inaugurated with considerable fanfare as a result of public will.

"It appears as if the *people*," reported the *Intelligencer*, "actuated by a general and spontaneous impulse, determined to manifest, in the strangest manner the interest excited by this great event, and their conviction of the close connection between it and their happiness."

Citizens from adjacent and even remote states had been pouring into Washington, straining the town's small capacity of accommodation and filling the streets. Early on the morning of March 4, a Saturday, salutes were fired from the Naval Yard and from nearby Fort Washington, and the Washington volunteer militia assembled. There was such eagerness by the public to witness the swearing-in ceremony that the new hall at the House of Representatives was filled to capacity and overflowing several hours before noon. The crowd surrounding the Capitol was estimated at ten thousand.

Shortly before noon, Madison was met at his house by an escort of mounted Washington and Georgetown militia and escorted in his carriage to the Capitol. Madison wore a suit which, significantly, was manufactured locally from wool of Merino sheep raised in the United States. This was a proud reflection of America's growing mercantile capacity.

Madison was met at the House chamber by Jefferson, his good friend who had ridden by horseback from the White House. After taking the oath and addressing Congress, Madison was saluted with two rounds of artillery fire as he exited the building. Nine companies of volunteer militia in full uniform were drawn into formation and passed in review.

Afterward, the militia escorted him back to his home, where he was called upon by well-wishers, among them ex-President Jefferson. The callers enjoyed refreshments and socialized until, taking their cue from the departure of Jefferson, they too said their farewells.

Another element of presidential inauguration was reinstated that night when a grand ball was held at Long's Hotel. Toasted as the "most brilliant and crowded affair ever known in Washington," it was attended by both Madison and Jefferson. The *Intelligencer* saw the happy fête as a harbinger of much good for the country.

Though the nation was at war with England in 1813, Madison's second inauguration followed much the same pattern as the first. The event was described as solemn and truly republican. Madison was escorted from the White House up Pennsylvania to the Capitol by volunteer cavalry troops and met on the Capitol grounds by the militia corps and the Marine Band. Afterward he was returned in similar fashion to the White House, where he and Dolley received visitors. A "splendid assembly" was held that night at Davis' Hotel with the president attending.

The Capitol was still under repair from its destruction by the British when James Monroe was inaugurated in 1817. This ceremony was much the same as Madison's except for one major difference. After taking the oath in the partially restored Senate chamber, Monroe was led to an elevated portico which had been erected for the occasion at the east entrance. There, instead of speaking only to Congress and a gallery audience, the president-elect made his address to the crowd outside. It was apparent that Americans increasingly harkened to the ceremony as a symbol of nation and unity.

With the House chamber back in use in 1821, President Monroe addressed Congress from a raised platform inside the chamber. The public's interest in the inaugural had not waned, and a great crowd filled the gallery, halls, and grounds to witness the ceremony, which was "characterized by simple grandeur and splendid simplicity . . ."

The election of 1824 uniquely presented four candidates, all of whom claimed to be "republican." Republicanism, however, had come to mean different things to different people. None of the candidates had any sort of party organization to support him. John Quincy Adams, who was eventually named president by the House of Representatives, had close ties to the rich industrial and commercial class of the East. As a result, his inauguration in 1825 was somewhat more regal and formal than preceding ones.

Among those congratulating Adams afterward was the man he had barely defeated for the office, General Andrew Jackson. Jackson represented a strong development of a new democratic, anti-class attitude throughout the nation. At the lead of this upsurge of the common man, Jackson easily defeated Adams in 1828. His inauguration the following March reflected a new grass-roots attitude toward the presidency and government. The day of knee breeches, silver buckles, and ruffles had ended.

By midmorning of inauguration day, the dirt streets of Washington were overflowing with carriages, wagons, and carts of every kind, many carrying men, women, and children whose dress indicated they ranged from the wealthy to the very poor. They thronged to the Capitol in such immense numbers that Jackson

After the inauguration of Andrew Jackson in 1829, "all creation" of citizens swarmed to the White House to celebrate a new day of democracy in America.

was forced to climb over a wall and enter the Capitol through the basement.

When the president-elect made his appearance on the east portico, he was greeted by an enormous roar. Then when he finished and bowed, the huge crowd swarmed forward en masse to congratulate him. Jackson attempted to escape through the Capitol and down the west front, but the crowd again blocked his way.

Finally a path was cleared, and the Tennessean mounted a horse and made his way to the White House.

Enticed by the promise of barrels of orange punch at the White House, the rambunctious crowd surged down Pennsylvania in pursuit of Jackson. Backwoodsmen, farmers, women, children, white and black, mounted and unmounted alike descended upon the president's home. The scene was to become a part of inaugural legend. The *Intelligencer* put it as kindly as it could:

"At the mansion of the President, the Sovereign People were a little uproarious, indeed, but it was anything but a malicious spirit."

Martin Van Buren considered himself a disciple of Jefferson and had served in Jackson's cabinet. Yet his inaugural in 1837 was marked by pageantry and formal protocol. Thus, in the wake of the Jacksonian era, acceptance of a more flaunted ceremony returned. The New Yorker's personal urbane taste was undoubtedly largely responsible, but mounting evidence of popular fondness for the event was undoubtedly a factor.

The cost of arrangements for the Van Buren inauguration was said to far exceed any of those previously held. Well-orchestrated by a committee for arrangements, it featured the dragoon escort of Jackson and Van Buren to the Capitol shortly before noon, a public address by the president-elect on the east portico, the taking of the oath, and then a cortege-attended procession to the White House. That night the president and vice president along with government, military, and foreign dignitaries attended an inaugural ball at Carusi's dancing academy, Eleventh and C streets.

The Van Buren ceremony, however, was outdone considerably in 1841 by that of William Henry Harrison, candidate of the Whig party. The old soldier, hero of the American victory over Indian forces under Tecumseh at Tippecanoe, had been elected by a wide margin as a favorite of "the People." Still, his inaugural was the most lavish Americans had yet witnessed.

Abraham Lincoln delivered his first inaugural address to a fearful nation that faced certain Civil War.

The president-elect, himself mounted on a white charger, was escorted from his quarters to the Capitol by a large array of marshals, military units, brass bands, and political and professional clubs carrying banners. There was even a delegation of Georgetown college students and faculty who displayed a large silk banner bearing the image of a golden eagle.

A vehicle drawn by six white horses, all fancily adorned and wearing bells, featured a display of weaving apparatus, which was operated as it went. Another exhibited a large log cabin, its sides emblazoned with mottos and its roof lined with flags of the states which had voted for General Harrison.

Visitors had been pouring into Washington and Georgetown for several days. As the procession moved down Pennsylvania Avenue toward the Capitol, thousands of people along the street cheered enthusiastically. Women waved handkerchiefs from the windows on both sides of the avenue, while other spectators watched from elevated platforms or atop roofs.

Among the enormous crowd surrounding the Capitol were women bedecked with bright-colored shawls and fluttering fans, top-hatted gentlemen with their fashionable canes, children carrying small banners displaying a log cabin and "Hero of Tippecanoe," knots of black people in their Sunday dress, military officers whose gold epaulets sparkled against their blue uniforms, and masses of others who roared their delight at Harrison's arrival.

Harrison delivered a lengthy address and took the oath. Cannons boomed, and the elaborate procession reformed to escort the new president to the White House. The huge crowd followed behind and soon filled the mansion to overflowing. Many people were unable to get inside. That night the inaugural event was further enlarged by the holding of several balls around Washington. Harrison paid his respects at each of them briefly.

During or soon after his inauguration, Harrison caught a cold that developed into pneumonia. Only one month after taking office, on April 4, the native Virginian and one-time governor of Indiana Territory died at the White House. However, despite his brief ten-

In 1881 newly inaugurated President James A. Garfield returned to the White House through a Grand Arch on Fifteenth Street next to the Treasury building. A temporary structure, it no longer exists.

ure in office, Harrison had helped firmly establish the inaugural ceremony as a popular symbol of American nationalism.

From his time on, the inaugural would continue to grow in pageantry and official protocol. Though at times affected by individual personalities and circumstances of history, the presidential inauguration had become an integral part of the American political system and still another vital symbol of national synthesis. Significantly, every four years it becomes a spotlight that focuses the attention of the nation and the world upon the capital of the United States.

One of the most memorable lines of inaugural speech was delivered by President John F. Kennedy in 1961: "Ask not what your country can do for you—ask what you can do for your country."

The Washington Monument

———

5

☆ Normally on the Fourth of July in Washington, the people in the public offices and others sought to flee the hot, dusty town with its wearying rattle of drums and annoying boom of cannon that had become a standard part of the annual celebration. But Independence Day of 1848 was different.

A drenching rain had fallen the previous morning, cooling the air and the city. A bright, clear sky gave promise to this being an especially fortunate day on which to celebrate the nation's seventy-second year of existence—and to lay the cornerstone for a monument in honor of the country's greatest hero and first president, George Washington.

The sound of bells ringing their carillon had awakened the town to a festive mood, and there followed salutes from the Naval Yard and Arsenal, the discharge of private firearms by citizens, and the pop-pop-pop of children's firecrackers. Adding to this were the stirring tattoo of drums and the brave call of bugles, all of which excited a patriotic fervor throughout the city.

Even as these early sounds were echoing from building to building, the streets were filled with people moving briskly about in preparation for the day's celebration. Temperance society squads, carrying their multicolored banners and emblems, hurried to their assigned parade locations—even as did carts loaded with hogsheads of beer.

Sunday School children, their faces aglow with excitement, danced in glee behind their tutors. Clattering and clanging along with splendid fury came a fire wagon, gleaming with polished brass and exhibiting a huge brass eagle on top. The wagon, preceded by young boys bearing torches, was drawn by long lines of manly firemen adorned in red jackets and white pantaloons.

Soon the streets of the city came alive with spectators moving along in happy anticipation. The normal public conveyances quickly proved inadequate for the enormous crowd. Extra railcars, even extra trains, were added to handle the influx of visitors who arrived to spread themselves with rapturous delight over the city. They asked residents and one another where was the president's house, where was the Patent Office, and where were all the other historic locations of their national capital about which they had heard and read. A *National Intelligencer* reporter described the scene:

> It were long to tell of the many bright-ribboned country bonnets which bustled and swayed about in the crowd, like poppy-heads shaken by the wind. It were harder to describe the thousand youthful, yes, and infantine faces, so full of raised earnestness—the round eye, the open mouth, the dumpling hands clinging to Mother's dress, or thrown about Father's neck and supporting arms.

The gathering point for the parade was at the military mustering grounds in front of City Hall at Fourth and D Street. It was a sight which defied simple description—of military squadrons in full plume, prancing cavalry horses and be-sabered officers, fire companies, orders of Masonic and temperance groups, carriages loaded with dignitaries, military colors flashing, bayonets and rifle barrels sparkling in the morning sun. Brass bands fell into formation and began tuning up. From upper-story windows, people leaned forward to wave and call out or to catch a glimpse of military heroes who had recently returned from battles in the war with Mexico.

Presently the order of march was formed, a signal shot was fired, and the procession began moving down Indiana to Pennsylvania. Then, with banners flying and music resounding, it followed up that parade avenue through walls of cheering spectators to the Treasury building at Fourteenth, turning abruptly southward. The procession numbered more than four thousand and stretched over a mile and a half along the route as it made its way to where the first stone for the Washington Monument awaited.

The marble block, weighing 2,500 pounds, had been quarried and presented to the Washington Monument Society by a Baltimore quarrier. Matthew G. Emery, who would later serve as a Washington mayor, had cut and dressed the stone. Earlier, on June 6, when the weighty block was being carted to the monument site, it had broken through the canal bridge at Fourteenth Street and fallen into the "stream of filth" that flowed there. It was rescued by workmen from the Naval Yard.

In a hollow close by the monument site, awning-covered seats had been placed to receive the honored guests of the day. These included government and military notables, emissaries of foreign countries, representatives from states and territories, and a delegation of Cherokee, Chickasaw, Stockbridge, Creek, and Choctaw Indians from the Indian Territory. The Cherokees and Chickasaws, who had been removed from their Southern homes to the distant Indian Territory, had donated liberally to the monument fund.

Among the dignitaries were ninety-one-year-old Mrs. Alexander Hamilton and Dolley Madison, eighty but still stately and stylishly different in her turban headpiece. Present also were Mrs. John Quincy Adams; former-President Martin Van Buren; future

The laying of the cornerstone of the Washington Monument on July 4, 1848, was a gala affair.

president Millard Fillmore; the recent President of the Republic of Texas and now-Senator Sam Houston; and others.

An attractive arch, wrapped in colorful cotton, had been erected. Atop it perched a live American eagle whose snowy head and tail and dark plumage gave emphasis to his piercing gaze. The forty-year-old bird was the same which the city of Alexandria had used to greet General Lafayette in 1824.

The undulating Mall, greened and cooled by the rain, was covered with carriages and by an estimated fifteen to twenty thousand people as the thunder of artillery and pealing of bells finally stilled and the ceremony began. President James K. Polk was present to hear The Hon. Robert C. Winthrop, Speaker of the House and the appointed orator of the day, give the principal address. Winthrop was replacing former-President John Quincy Adams, who had died on February 23 after suffering a stroke on the floor of the House of Representatives two days before. Winthrop noted:

> The Government of the country has not been unmindful of what it owes to Washington. One tribute to his memory is left to be rendered . . . a National monument, erected by the Citizens of the United States of America . . . Of such a monument we have come to lay the corner-stone . . . The place is appropriate . . . [here] on the banks of his own beloved and beautiful Potomac.

When Winthrop had finished, the Master of the Masonic order exercised his time-honored privilege. He took his position on the cornerstone and consecrated it with the standard Masonic ceremony. Fittingly, the same gavel that had been made especially for President Washington in laying the foundation stone of the Capitol building in 1793 was used.

Note was made of the large collection of materials which had been placed in a recess of the cornerstone: copies of the Declaration of Independence and the Constitution, a painting of George Washington, maps, city guides, books of poetry, all the coins of the United States from the eagle to the half-dime, flags, census records, the Washington family coat of arms, government documents, the Holy Bible, Morse's *North American Atlas*, magazines, illustrated catalogs, daguerreotypes of Washington and his wife, a cent piece of 1783 and specimens of Continental money, letters by national leaders, newspapers from numerous cities of thirteen states and the District of Columbia, and many other items of record and memorabilia.

A fireworks display by the Naval Yard awed the spectators

before the procession reformed and marched back up the original route to the Willard Hotel at Fourteenth and Pennsylvania, where the troops were reviewed by President Polk. The day of celebration was ended with a reception by the president in the East Room of the White House.

There had been interest from the very start in erecting a suitable memorial to Washington. Many people were not satisfied with mere statuary; they wanted a more significant tribute to the great man. In 1833, a group of prominent citizens met in Washington, D.C., and formed the Washington National Monument Society.

John Marshall, then seventy-eight, was named president. When he died two years later, he was followed by James Madison, then by Andrew Jackson. When, in 1836, the Society advertised for submissions of a monument design, it was Robert Mills's obelisk shaft concept that was chosen.

With the support of the federal government, the Society set about to secure a site for the edifice. L'Enfant's original site where the city's east-west, north-south lines met at the west end of the Mall was a unanimous choice. However, the advantages of an elevated spot a hundred yards to the southeast won out over L'Enfant's precise symmetrical point.

Various fund-raising methods were employed by the Society. Lithograph prints of the Mills obelisk were given to persons contributing a dollar or more. When this system produced modest results, prints of a George Washington portrait were added. For eight dollars, a contributor would receive large prints of both Washington and the monument; for five dollars, a large print of only Washington; for a dollar and a half, small prints of both; and for a dollar, a small print of the monument.

By 1847, $87,000 had been raised, and the laying of the cornerstone was scheduled for Washington's birthday, February 22, 1848. However, for weather considerations it was postponed until July 4. The euphoric celebration of laying the cornerstone launched the construction of the obelisk, but in a form modified from the original Mills plan. Mills's obelisk shaft was at variance with traditional concepts, and it was altered to produce a classical shape void of obtrusive decoration or embellishment, more on the design of an Egyptian obelisk.

Now, however, donations lagged badly, partially because of the growing antagonism between North and South over the issue of slavery. Appeals to Congress, to banks, and even to schoolchildren around the country produced little revenue. A fund-raising program held at the base of the monument on July 4, 1850, was a dismal failure. Lack of interest and excessive heat prevented a planned military and civic procession.

President Zachary Taylor attended the ceremony and saw the city of Washington present a beautiful cut of white marble to the monument. It was to be Taylor's last public event, for a few days later he died, either of exposure to heat and acute indigestion from overeating or from cholera.

In 1854, work on the Washington Monument ceased, its shaft having reached only 150 feet above ground. Depletion of funds and quarrels over control of the Society's records were to blame. But a disagreeable incident also added to the monument controversy. It concerned a marble stone which had been donated to the Monument Society by the Pope. The stone had once stood in the Temple of Concord at Rome.

Early on a morning in March, 1854, a band of anti-foreign, anti-Catholic members of the Know-Nothing party came to the monument area, locked up the night watchman, poisoned his dog, and carted off the stone. It was thought that, after defacing the "Pope's Stone," they dumped it over a steep bank into the Potomac River.

Yokes of oxen were used to haul the heavy stone blocks as construction of the Washington Monument progressed in 1854.

For twenty-five years, the monument to Washington stood blunted and ugly on the landscape of the capital city. Far from being a gracious tribute to America's national hero and a symbol of unity, the unfinished stack of stone blocks gave testimony to the bitterness and rancor of a nation divided. Its surrounding sward, so pleasant in 1848, was now littered with stone blocks and debris.

During the Civil War it was occupied by herds of cattle and, even, a slaughterhouse. To the west the smelly, unhealthy slough was a threat to the foundation of the monument as well as a repugnant, offensive blight.

Efforts in behalf of the monument had been continued by private groups such as Masonic wives and daughters who, during a national Masonic meeting in Chicago, formed the Ladies' National Washington Monument Association. Its purpose was to aid the cause of the Monument Society by assisting in raising funds. A *Harper's Magazine* essayist visiting the capital in 1868 noted:

"The Washington Monument . . . still raises its unfinished shaft of marble into the air, the funds for which are exhausted; and wherever you go a little model of it as it should be presents itself as a glass money-box to your notice . . ."

Bills submitted to Congress in the tribute's behalf failed, but individual states now stepped forward with financial help. In 1871, the New York legislature appropriated $10,000 toward construction of the monument. This was followed by Minnesota with one thousand, New Jersey with three thousand, and Connecticut with two thousand. Contribution boxes installed in public offices during the 1876 centennial celebration netted $90,000 in subscriptions.

Meanwhile, Senator John Sherman of Ohio offered a resolution

It is still possible to see the line where the work on the Washington Monument stopped in 1854, not to begin again until 1880.

to Congress for the federal government to appropriate $100,000 to continue construction of the Washington Monument. This figure was upped to $200,000 by a House bill after a compromise was reached dividing the sum into four equal annual payments. Now the Corps of Engineers would take over construction. The act was signed into law by President Ulysses S. Grant on August 2, 1876, though it would be 1880 before actual work would resume.

A serious engineering problem had now presented itself. It was calculated that the old foundation, built of bluestone gneiss, would not support the huge structure. Already the shaft was slightly out of plumb, its axis leaning two and one-quarter inches to the north. Further, the top of the shaft was found not to be exactly square.

By widening and deepening the foundation area and filling in with masses of concrete, an entirely new base support was provided. The imperfection in the shaft's squareness was corrected gradually until, with a slight twist, it had disappeared within fifty feet of the top.

On August 7 of that year, President Rutherford B. Hayes ascended by elevator to the 150-foot elevation where cement had been poured for a new stone marker. Hayes placed into the cement a small coin on which his initials and the date were scratched. Others of his party followed suit and the stone was lowered onto the concrete bed and work commenced.

Once again the obelisk began rising against the Washington skyline, and observers watched its progress daily from the windows and steps of the Capitol and White House. Maryland marble was used to face the remainder of the shaft. Coming from different stratum than the original stone, it left a slight ring at the 150-foot level.

The capstone of the Washington Monument was put in place on December 6, 1884, thirty-six years after the original cornerstone had been laid.

Lining the inside of the Monument at various levels were some 190 stones donated by states, territories, cities, Indian tribes, societies, individuals, and foreign nations—among them being China, Japan, Switzerland, Egypt, Siam, Brazil, Turkey, Wales, and Greece. The inscription on the stone from China read:

> It was evident that Washington was a remarkable man. He extended the frontiers thousands of miles, then refused to usurp the regal dignity or transmit it to his posterity, but first established rules for an elective administration. Where in the world can be found such a public spirit? . . . Ah! who would not call him a hero?

By August 9, 1884, the walls of the shaft had reached the 500-foot level. A laborious iron, crisscross, inside stairway was supplemented by a steam hoist elevator as the masons worked their way higher and higher. Rising to a height of 555 feet, the structure was believed to be the tallest in the world at the time. Only the Biblical Tower of Babel, it was said, had ever surpassed it.

At long last, on December 6, the grand finale of construction was undertaken when the aluminum capstone—the largest block of that metal that had yet been cast—was set in place atop the shaft. Above it was mounted the Stars and Stripes of the United States. It was time to commemorate the long-delayed achievement and to celebrate.

The ceremonies were set for February 21, 1885. The day was clear and cold, and a light snow had fallen during the night. A whipping wind and the low temperature made the occasion far less joyous than had been the original dedication thirty-seven years before. Still, a large crowd turned out early, many of them hugging

Stones from many countries, organizations, states, lodges, schoolchildren, and Indian tribes were among the building blocks of the Washington Monument when it was dedicated February 21, 1885.

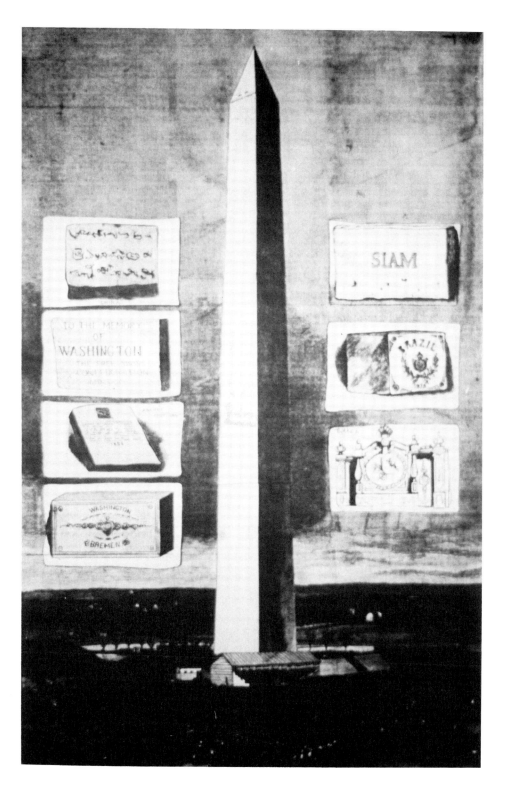

the leeward side of buildings against the bitter cold, to witness the proceedings which began at the monument.

With Senator Sherman presiding, prayers were offered. These were followed by addresses from Washington capitalist W. W. Corcoran and others. President Chester A. Arthur formally received the monument and dedicated it "to the immortal name and memory of George Washington."

This concluded, a large procession of military and civic groups formed under General Philip Sheridan and marched to the Capitol. There more ceremony was conducted, including the reading of a speech for Robert C. Winthrop, who had made the principal address in 1848 but was now too ill to do so again. Music was presented by the U.S. Marine Band, orations were made, and a benediction given.

In the evening a magnificent fireworks display was held at the foot of the monument, including one depicting Washington on horseback. And when darkness came, spectators gasped in awe when the north face of the great marble shaft was illuminated with powerful lights of various colors.

At long last the nation had paid honor to the man whom most Americans accept as their greatest hero. It had done so with an edifice of force and visual beauty, one that would merit the admiration and appreciation of future generations.

Mount Vernon:
A National Shrine

6

☆ Throughout the course of United States history, the home and burial site of George Washington at Mount Vernon, Virginia, has been looked upon as a national shrine. No one man more than Washington represents the common struggle of the American colonies for independence and the ideal of union.

Throughout the Revolutionary War, it was he who had welded together and led the meager American military forces against the mighty British armies. And once the war was won, it was Washington who was looked to as the man—and possibly the only man—who, as the first president, could prevent the tremulous union of states from cracking apart.

When Washington had hesitated to accept the nomination for a second term, Thomas Jefferson had encouraged him by noting: "North and South will hang together while they have you to hang to."

Thus, it was not surprising that the nation would venerate Washington's home and burial site at Mount Vernon. He had inherited the Virginia plantation at the age of twenty-two. Through

During colonial times, George Washington enjoyed the life of a country gentleman at his Virginia estate home of Mount Vernon.

his successful management, the estate prospered and provided him with the life of a successful stockman and farmer.

He experimented in stock breeding and agricultural techniques, operating gardens and greenhouses for experiments with new varieties of seeds and plants. The Mount Vernon plantation produced flour and tobacco principally, though barrels of shad and herring taken from the Potomac were also shipped out to foreign ports. Washington was a slaveholder, but he disapproved of the practice and sought a way to end it.

His life was much that of a country squire, which included

dancing, horse racing, cockfighting, and fox chases over the Virginia countryside in the English tradition. In sharp contrast to this were the hardships and privations he knew in serving with General Edward Braddock during the French and Indian War and leading the American armies through a long and difficult war.

Washington twice enlarged the Mount Vernon home, which held a majestic hilltop view some 200 feet above the Potomac River. He was personally responsible for the layout and landscaping of the Mount Vernon grounds. When called away to soldier or to serve in government, Washington sorely missed his beloved Mount Vernon.

He died in his own bedroom there on December 14, 1799, and was buried, as he had directed, in the family vault on the site. Immediately afterward, on December 24, Congress passed a resolution for the erection of a monument at Washington, D.C., under which Washington's body would be placed. Accordingly, a request was made of his wife, Martha, for the removal of Washington's body from Mount Vernon. She gave her consent, graciously replying:

"Taught by the great example which I have so long had before me never to oppose my private wishes to the public will, I need not, I cannot say what a sacrifice of individual feeling I make to a sense of public duty."

Having secured this agreement, in 1800 Congress passed a bill appropriating $200,000 for the construction of a mausoleum in Washington City. Nothing was done, however, and the project lay in limbo until 1824 when a resolution to look into the matter was presented in the House by Representative James Buchanan. Buchanan expressed concern that the government had not lived up to the pledge it had made to Martha Washington.

The memory of Washington was reawakened in the public that same year when the Marquis de Lafayette and his son, George Washington Lafayette, visited America. The Frenchman, who had served at Washington's side during the Revolutionary War, was much admired by many Americans.

Traveling by steamboat down the river from Washington in October, 1824, Lafayette paid an emotional visit to Mount Vernon. It was there that forty years before he had said farewell to the great American he so admired and loved.

Lafayette was met by George Washington Parke Custis, the adopted son of the first president. After touring the Washington home, Lafayette was led to the family burial vault where a short ceremony of remembrance was held. Lafayette entered the vault and kissed Washington's tomb. In 1831, a new burial vault was finally built on a site that Washington himself had selected before he died.

On February 12, 1837, a joint committee of Congress considered a recommendation to place the resolution of 1799 into effect and have Washington's body moved to the Capitol and interred in a vault beneath the rotunda. It was ultimately decided, however, that to do so would be contrary to the express wishes of Washington's will that he be buried at Mount Vernon.

The years passed, and hard times fell upon the estate. The place became badly run-down, and the home and other buildings were falling apart. It wasn't until 1853 that much interest in Mount Vernon was activated. The threat of secession by Southern states over the issue of slavery initiated a desire by some Americans to search for symbols of common ground between North and South that would serve the cause of national unity.

Mount Vernon was seen as an obvious candidate. Not only was it the home and burial site of Washington, but it was located in Virginia. A national shrine in a Southern state would be especially valuable.

Still, little was achieved until the wife of a wealthy South Carolina planter, while on a boat trip up the Potomac, caught sight of Mount Vernon standing derelict and decaying on the riverbank.

She was dismayed and deeply saddened at the sight. Her daughter, Ann Pamela Cunningham, learned of the home's condition and took up the cause of restoration of Mount Vernon.

She began writing letters to newspapers appealing to Southern women and organized The Daughters of Washington in 1854. Ac-

George Washington said farewell to his comrade-in-arms, the Marquis de Lafayette, at Mount Vernon in 1784.

tress/playwright Ann Coran Mowatt also took up the cause, turning it into a national movement under the Mount Vernon Ladies' Association of the Union. The women felt they were working for more than simply restoring Mount Vernon. They believed they were serving the great hope which Washington often declared for "an indissoluble union."

Edward Everett, the famous Boston orator and statesman, spoke eloquently on the matter throughout both the North and South. By his efforts some $70,000 was raised toward the purchase of Mount Vernon by the Mount Vernon Ladies' Association in 1858.

A descriptive writer for *Harper's New Monthly Magazine* made a trip to Mount Vernon in 1859 for the express purpose of seeing it before remodeling took place. Interestingly, he was met at the dock by a young daguerreotypist who was passing out handbills encouraging visitors to have their likeness made in front of Washington's tomb.

The Washington family tomb was in bad disarray. Vandals had broken into it, and some of the bodies had been disturbed. Washington's tomb was untouched; but now a descendant of the first president ordered the coffin opened for inspection. By the dim light of the candles, it appeared that Washington's body had deteriorated little over the years.

While at Mount Vernon, the writer was shown a copy of a drawing made by Washington of the position of the trees he had ordered planted along the walkways. Many of the trees were still standing at the time, and some are there today. The journalist also met a former slave named Westford, who had lived there since 1796 and who told many interesting tales of earlier days.

The *Harper's* scribe wrote of the many personal artifacts of Mount Vernon. One of the more intriguing was the handsome Spanish dress sword which Washington wore as president. It had originally been presented in 1757 by a French duchess to Benjamin Franklin, who bequeathed it to Washington. On one side of the

The Washington tomb at Mount Vernon has long been a revered shrine for Americans.

blade was inscribed *Recte Face Ice,* "Do what is right"; and on the other side, *Nemine Timeas,* "Fear no man."

But upon nearly everything of the mansion itself, the visitor noted, there were signs of decay. Not one hour was to be lost, he insisted, if Mount Vernon were to be restored to its former beauty.

Further attention was drawn to the Washington home in 1860 by the visit of the Prince of Wales, then nineteen and later to become King Edward VII of Great Britain. Traveling by steamboat down the Potomac from Washington City, the young Prince and his party paid their respects to Washington's tomb.

"There is something grandly suggestive," an English journal commented, "of historical retribution in the reverential awe of the Prince of Wales, the great-grandson of George III, standing bareheaded at the foot of the coffin of Washington."

Like most other things in America at the time, the restoration of Mount Vernon was interrupted by the Civil War. By 1874, it could be reported that the Mount Vernon Ladies' Association had made a great many improvements. Still, much remained to be done. Revenue for the project was being raised from the daily line of boats bringing tourists to Mount Vernon.

But the entrance fees and sales of souvenirs on the grounds were not enough. A proposal had been made that each of the original thirteen states of the Union take up the work of refurbishing a room of the mansion.

Today, Mount Vernon stands fully restored and served by the Mount Vernon Memorial Highway, only sixteen miles from downtown Washington, D.C. It is visited by thousands of tourists every year. Those who walk the beautiful, treed grounds and take the tour through the restored mansion join a long parade of others who have been coming here for generations.

Mount Vernon has been saved from the erosion of time. But its symbolic message is equally important. There are those who pray that the site will continue to remind Americans of Washington the man, of his struggle for an independent nation, and his undying hope for a unified America.

Today the Mount Vernon shrine is kept in immaculate condition for the thousands of tourists who visit it annually.

National Buildings, Parks, and Statuary

7

☆ In the European tradition, the capital of a great nation must have its Capitol and its kingly palace. But these alone were not enough. They required other noble architecture and landscaped areas over which they could reign. Further, a great nation required idealistic ennoblement of its accomplishments. What better way was there to bind a nation together than by uniting the people in veneration of their heroes?

L'Enfant's plan provided for intervening "play houses, rooms of assembly, academies" between the Capitol and executive mansion. Also, at key intersections throughout his envisioned city, the spacious landscape would display "statues, columns, and obelisks" plus other ornaments to honor the country's civic and military leaders. In these concepts, L'Enfant had wisely foreseen the incorporation of theaters, public buildings, cultural centers, parks, and statues as essential elements of the city.

The first two government office buildings to be erected were the Treasury building just east of the White House and the War Department building on the west. These twin structures featured dormer windows in the roof and outside steps leading to the first floor above a raised freestone basement. Neither of the red brick buildings was particularly impressive; they were simply all the government could then afford.

Congress had wanted these building erected close to the Capitol so it could keep an eye on their operations. President Washington objected, insisting that they were for year-round operation while the Congress met only part-time. He personally attended the staking out of the sites in October, 1796.

The Treasury building was begun in 1798 and occupied in 1800. In 1805, during Jefferson's administration, Latrobe began the building of a fireproof vault, beginning at the Treasury and extending toward the White House. Eventually the two buildings were connected by a stone bridge. The War Department building was completed soon after the Treasury. These two structures served the government's needs until both were burned by the British in 1814. They had been rebuilt on their original sites by 1816.

In 1818, the two original buildings were joined by two more of the same design, one for the State Department and another for the Navy, making a boxed area around the White House. It was originally planned to dress the front of all four with freestone porticos supported by six Ionic columns. However, the porticos were added only to the north front of the two new buildings.

In 1833, the Treasury again burned. It was replaced at the same site by a much longer building, designed by architect Robert Mills. Washingtonians were dismayed to find that the new three-story structure extended along Fifteenth Street into Pennsylvania Avenue, interrupting the visual link with the Capitol.

The Mills design, with flourishing long walls of Ionic columns, was completed in 1840. Later, it was extended even farther onto the course of Pennsylvania by the addition of an expanded new front on its south end.

In 1856, the State Department building remained tucked in at

The original State Department building, erected west of the White House in 1818, stood for many years at the north end of the new Treasury building.

the north end of the overwhelming Treasury. On the west, the War and Navy structures still stood . . . "two venerable old two-story buildings of brick, painted blue, looking very much like a college or seminary in a country village."

These buildings were replaced by the State, War, and Navy building, a massive French Renaissance edifice begun in 1871 and completed in 1888. Its large, columned exterior walls provided the Washington of that period with a feeling of palatial luxury. Today, it is known as the Old Executive Office building.

Three other important government buildings extended the classic Grecian design along the north of Pennsylvania between the Capitol and White House. They were the Patent Office, City Hall, and the Post Office.

The Patent Office, commenced in 1836, featured bold Doric-columned porticos on three sides, the main entrance on the south being copied from the Parthenon. The wings of the large building were of glistening white marble. Facing south on F Street between

The third Treasury building, redesigned by Robert Mills, features long exterior walls of Ionic columns.

Eighth and Ninth streets, it was completed just before the Civil War. Today it houses the Tariff Commission.

Construction on the City Hall, facing D Street between Fourth and Fifth, began in 1820. Though it distorted L'Enfant's plan for the location of municipal functions, the classical Grecian Ionic structure added much to the beauty of Washington architecture. The building now houses the U.S. District Court, and the area surrounding it is known as Judiciary Square.

The three-story, Corinthian-style Post Office, fronting on E Street between Seventh and Eighth streets, was erected after the old building had burned in 1839. Constructed of white marble, its front featured a center tympanum and two wings with a series of Corinthian pilasters (flat columns) on the upper two stories. This building, now gone, was replaced in 1934 by a Doric-columned structure at Pennsylvania and Twelfth Street.

From the very beginning of American independence, there had been hopes of establishing a national museum. For a number of years, a museum of sorts was housed on the second floor of the Patent Office. Among the items on display there were the uniform, camp chest, sword, and other relics of George Washington. Its most valuable prize, however, was the original copy of the Declaration of Independence, which is now far more securely protected in the National Archives in Washington.

In 1829, English scientist James Smithson willed his entire fortune to the United States—providing his nephew died without an heir. The fund was to be used to found a "Smithsonian Institution" dedicated to the increase and diffusion of knowledge among men. When the nephew obligingly died in 1835 without producing any children, there began a long debate in Congress over whether the money should be accepted and how it should be managed.

By this time, the bequest had grown from its original $550,000 to $750,000. In 1844, Congress accepted a design for the building from James Renwick, a style that departed severely from Grecian

The Smithsonian's turreted red sandstone castle was completed in 1858, the first of the Institution's many showcases for our national treasures of science and art.

classic. Renwick's design was a turreted Norman castle of red sandstone.

It wasn't until 1847 that a site for the building on the south side of the Mall was agreed upon and eleven years more before the structure was completed. Its location had honored L'Enfant's concept of the Mall, but in the opinion of many the building did little to enhance the capital's beauty.

Today the Smithsonian is a vast complex of museums and art

galleries, research facilities, and the National Zoo. Stretching along the sides of the Mall are the Museum of American History, the Museum of Natural History, the National Air and Space Museum, the Hirshhorn Museum, the Arts and Industries Building, the Freer Gallery, the Arthur M. Sackler Gallery, the Museum of African Art, as well as the original Smithsonian building. The Smithsonian is closely associated with the National Gallery of Art, also on the Mall, and the Kennedy Center for the Performing Arts. Its National Portrait Gallery and three other museums are elsewhere in the city.

The Columbian Institute had fostered the formation of a private scientific group in 1817, the Washington Botanical Society. Congress gave the Society six acres of land at the foot of Capitol Hill for a Botanic Garden such as Washington had suggested for the nation in 1796. Still, the group was stymied by lack of money, and difficulties created by the swamplands along the Washington Canal discouraged activity for several years.

Finally, in 1849, Congress voted funds to build a greenhouse at the west foot of Capitol Hill and move the Botanic Garden from where it had been located in the Patent Office to the new location. The Garden featured a central 55-foot-high glass dome with two smaller octagonal wings extending east and west. It soon became a favorite with visiting tourists and townspeople alike. There could be seen towering palms, rare ferns, and many other exotic plants from the far regions of the world.

Congress first established the Library of Congress in 1800 when it appropriated $5,000 for the purchase of books and set up the Library in the Capitol building. After the British destroyed it when they burned the Capitol, Congress accepted the offer of Thomas Jefferson to sell his personal 6,700-volume collection for $23,700.

Another fire destroyed the Library's quarters in the Capitol and all but 20,000 books in 1851. It wasn't until 1886 that a building designed expressly to house the Library was approved and eleven more years before it was completed. Its French Renaissance struc-

The original Botanic Garden was located directly west of the Capitol,
an area once so poorly kept that rubbish was dumped there.

President James K. Polk installed the statue of Thomas Jefferson that stood for many years on the north lawn of the White House.

ture followed the style of architecture prevalent at the time with a massive, highly ornate appearance.

Parks, squares, and circles were essential elements of the L'Enfant design, and his plan called for many. The three principal parks were those surrounding the Capitol and executive mansion and the Mall. Many others came into being over the years, largely subject to the commercial and residential development of the city. Some, however, have deep historical roots.

The President's Park—or The Common, as it was once known—was divided into three areas: the few acres for the White House itself; an area to the north, which became Lafayette Square; and the larger area to the south which sloped down to Tiber Creek bordering the Mall—today's Ellipse area.

On the Fourth of July during Jefferson's presidency, fairs would be held at the President's Park. Jefferson received a delegation of Cherokee chiefs there on July 4, 1801. It became customary on that day for vendors to set up around the square and sell wares, food, and drink. The public came in swarms to hold horse races, cockfights, and dogfights, and contests of manly skills. Often the militia drilled there in the evening while the president watched from the White House porch.

For many years, a statue of Jefferson stood on a pedestal of stuccoed brick inside a circular walk on the north of the White House. Placed there by President Polk in 1847, it was the only presidential statue to stand within the mansion grounds. In 1864, it was removed to Statuary Hall, where it remains today.

Lafayette Square gained its identity in 1825 when the Marquis de Lafayette visited the city during his American tour. After addressing a joint session of Congress, the French nobleman was given a military escort to the "court in front of the President's Mansion." Flower gardens were maintained in the park amid shady elms and perfumed magnolias.

The site became special when on January 8, 1853, the Clark Mills equestrian statue of Andrew Jackson was installed there. The statue gained much attention from Mills's feat of creating a balanced Jackson and rearing charger. Mills had wished to place a motto on the statue base: "The Federal Union, It Must Be Preserved." But the idea was rejected, many thought by then-Secretary of War Jefferson Davis.

Union soldiers camped at Lafayette Square during the Civil War. The park became badly run-down, its flower gardens turned into mires. Lafayette Square was restored under the administration of Ulysses S. Grant. Four statues of Europeans who assisted in the American Revolution were eventually installed in its corners: Lafayette in 1891; Comte de Rochambeau in 1902; the Polish General Thaddeus Kosciusko and General Baron von Steuben in 1910.

One of the earliest parks of the city was Franklin Square. At one time a bubbling spring existed there. In 1833, its water was piped through drilled-out logs to reservoirs at the White House for fire protection.

Mount Vernon Square, sitting at the intersection of New Jersey and Massachusetts avenues, was once the site of an early Washington maketplace known as the North Liberties Market. It was the scene of bloody conflict in 1857 when the U.S. Marines were called in to put down a riot caused by the radical Know-Nothing party. Six men were killed. In 1872, the market stalls were razed and the square cleared.

Farragut Square, containing a single block just northwest of the White House, features the bronze figure of Admiral David G. Farragut of Civil War fame. The statue, which was cast of metal taken from his flagship, the *Hartford*, was unveiled in 1881.

A controversial statue of George Washington had been completed by Horatio Greenough in 1843. The twenty-ton marble presented the figure of Washington loosely clad in a Roman toga, one arm holding a sword and a finger pointing skyward. Many people thought the likeness to be lifeless and ill-conceived. The statuary stood for many years on the east lawn of the Capitol before being moved to the rotunda in 1908 and later to the Smithsonian Institution.

Of the over 4,000 statues erected of Washington, one of the

The equestrian statue of President Andrew Jackson centers the famous Lafayette Square north of the White House.

more famous is that by Clark Mills. This equestrian memorial was unveiled at Washington Circle on Washington's birthday, 1860. Despite a pelting rain, the dedication featured an extended review of military units in honor of the man who more than any other represented a unified nation. Parading under the American colors were many officers and men who very soon would be facing one another in the deadly war of secession.

The post-Civil War period spawned numerous statues dedicated to outstanding men of that great conflict. Unquestionably, the most notable figure of the time had been President Abraham Lincoln. His two great accomplishments were the freeing of slaves and preservation of the Union. In 1876, a statue of him by Thomas Ball was unveiled at Lincoln Square.

The bronze figure depicts Abraham Lincoln with his hand resting on the shoulder of a crouching Negro. His other hand holds the Emancipation Proclamation, his historic document which freed the American slave.

There were many memorials erected to Civil War generals and admirals and others who followed. The multitude of statues, parks, squares, and circles of present Washington, D.C., bear the names of many American historical figures. Some would prove significant only to the day, some lasting for the ages. They all contribute to the total value of the capital as a national site for honoring the heroes of peace and war.

Among L'Enfant's visionary elements for the capital was a magnificent cascade of water 40-feet high and 100-feet wide in front of the Capitol building. This dream never materialized, and beautification of the Jenkins Hill pedestal was slow in coming.

During John Adams' administration, Capitol architect Charles Bulfinch obtained appropriations to fence and landscape the twenty acres of ground about the Capitol. Shrubs were planted and flower beds installed. But destruction of the Capitol in 1814 and the ensuing rebuilding years delayed development of the grounds.

In the spring of 1831, Congress voted funds for improvement of the Capitol Square grounds, particularly those on the west. The land was graded and cleared, shrubs and trees from Virginia and Maryland planted, and walks bordered with flowers. During the antebellum period, the Capitol grounds became a favorite resort for visitors.

People came in the cool of summer evenings to stroll the shaded grounds, enjoy the view from the lofty west portico, and listen to the Marine Band, which performed its airs there. Croquet was played on the east lawn.

The addition of wings and a new dome to the Capitol and the Civil War again disrupted the Capitol park. During the early 1870s, under the direction of Frederick Law Olmstead, Sr., the Capitol grounds were redesigned. The west front was terraced and the un-ruly forest there was cleared of decaying trees. Winding walks and much improved landscaping changed the "backyard" effect of the west front.

The Mall is one of the nation's oldest federal parks, though it languished for over a century before it finally came to realization. L'Enfant's esplanade, presenting its broad greensward westward from the Capitol, was a key element in his dream of a capital city. Despite its failure over the years to materialize, somehow the dream never died.

Even in 1861, the Mall was still a wasteland of untended swamps, split by the polluted, foul-smelling Washington Canal. Lumber sheds, coal yards, trash piles, and civic waste cluttered the banks of the canal. Its rubbish piles drew pigs, goats, and stray dogs, and insects infested the area. During the Civil War, it became the site of military camps and makeshift hospitals.

Buildings and railroads were permitted to intrude into the area. The Baltimore and Ohio Railroad tracks and depot (where President Garfield was shot in 1881) lay at the very foot of Capitol Hill. In 1873, after the canal was closed, the Baltimore and Potomac Railroad built its tracks from the south across the Mall to Pennsylvania. Its engine sheds and large depot were located where the National Gallery of Art stands today at Fourth and Constitution.

A portion of the Mall area was beautified with the landscaping of the Smithsonian grounds in 1855 and those of the Agriculture Department in 1868. Completion of the Washington Monument and improvement of its area also helped considerably. But it wasn't until 1901 that a plan to develop the Mall was initiated under the guidance of a special committee headed by Senator James Mc-Millan of Michigan.

An important part of this involved connecting the Capitol grounds and the east end of the Mall with a beautified plot that came to be known as Union Square.

The railroads were persuaded to remove from the Mall area as a first step. The Botanic Garden, which had sat squarely in front of the Capitol disrupting the view, and the Bartholdi Fountain (designed by the sculptor of the Statue of Liberty, Augustus Bartholdi) were moved to the south. Two monuments were set inside oval drives at the corners of the east end of the Mall.

Standing today on the northeast at Pennsylvania is the marble Peace or Naval Monument. Erected in 1877 in memory of Navy personnel lost at sea during the Civil War, it depicts the figure of *America* weeping on the shoulder of *History* for the loss of her heroic dead. The figures of *Mars* and *Neptune* are at her feet, while around the base are those of *Victory* and *Peace*.

On the southeast the Garfield Memorial was unveiled in 1887. The image of the assassinated President Garfield stands on a tall column surrounded by representations of him as a student, a soldier, and a statesman.

Centering the east end of the Mall along First Street is the Grant Memorial. One of the most costly pieces of statuary in the city, it displays a bronze of Grant as a Civil War general. Mounted on his horse, he commands groups of Union cavalry and artillery suspended in the dramatic action of war.

Attention was given to the west end of the Mall in 1897 when Congress set aside 621 acres of reclaimed flats and the 118 acres of tidal reservoir for Potomac Park. Ultimate realization of the L'Enfant grand esplanade would come during the nation's second century with a beautified Mall flanked by new government edifices and adorned by magnificent memorials.

National Memorials

———

8

In 1867, two years after the assassination of Abraham Lincoln, Congress appointed a commission for establishing a fitting memorial to the man who had saved the Union and freed the slaves. It was agreed that such a tribute should be one of the great national memorials, rivaling even the Washington Monument.

However, it would be over half a century before this momentous goal was achieved. In a way, this was fortunate. It permitted time to erase the bitter acrimony of the Civil War that dimmed the greatness of Lincoln. When the Lincoln Memorial was finally dedicated in 1922, it quickly became one of the nation's most admired and beloved shrines.

There was much indecision over the most appropriate way to honor the man who had saved the Union. Another statue—there were many such in cities around the nation—was not enough. Some wanted an obelisk similar to Washington's. Others a huge pyramid, a capital park, or a memorial highway.

The form of the memorial was decided when architect Henry

Bacon submitted his proposed design to the commission. It was a neoclassic version of a Greek Doric temple with a Roman-style attic. It was similar to the Parthenon except that the side presented the main facade and entrance.

The structure's central block would be surrounded by thirty-six Doric columns—one for each of the states of the Union at the time of Lincoln's death. The columns were to be tilted inward slightly to prevent the building from looking top-heavy. A grand sweep of steps would lead up to where a statue of Lincoln was displayed inside the peristyle porch of the classic Greek temple.

The assignment of producing the statue was awarded to Daniel Chester French, the most prominent American sculptor of the day. Creator of such American epic sculptures as *The Minute Man* at Lexington, Massachusetts, he undertook the assignment with great sensitivity to its historical significance.

French studied photographs and life masks of Lincoln, as well as plaster casts of his hands. From these he decided upon the image of a seated Lincoln. For six years French worked to reproduce the rugged-but-kindly face of the man who had most carried the burden of the Civil War. The hands, relaxed over the arms of his chair, reflected Lincoln's great moral strength.

Originally the statue was to be ten feet high. But French soon realized that it would need to be larger lest it be dwarfed by the building. Accordingly, it was almost doubled in size. Twenty-eight blocks of white Georgian marble, fitted together so tightly that the seams are barely visible, were required for the final carving from French's quarter-size model.

Determination of the most suitable site for the memorial was another problem. Many people believed that it should be tied in with the Capitol as an integral part of the national saga of a free and united people.

John Hay, Lincoln's secretary and biographer, insisted that the memorial should be located on a line with the Capitol and Wash-

Above: The inward-tilting columns of the Lincoln Memorial were designed to prevent the neoclassic edifice from appearing top-heavy.

Right: The heroic marble statue of the seated Lincoln in the Lincoln Memorial was created by Daniel Chester French, who spent six years working on it.

ington Monument, according to L'Enfant's original scheme. He wished for it to stand alone on the edge of the Potomac, removed from the business activity of the city, "isolated, distinguished and serene."

Hay's suggestion was followed. The area west of the Washing-

ton Monument that had once been marshy backwater of the Tidal Basin was drained and filled. On February 12, 1914, ground was broken, and foundation work began. Though slowed temporarily by World War I, work on the memorial continued steadily.

The statue of Lincoln by French, destined to be the greatest of them all, was completed and put into place in 1920. Now the area was landscaped with lawns, trees, shrubbery, roadways, and walks to produce a lush green backdrop for the majestic white edifice.

Work had begun, also, on the Reflecting Pool visually connecting the memorial with the Washington Monument. This was not yet completed on May 30, 1922, when Robert Todd Lincoln, son of the president, joined President Warren G. Harding, former president and then Chief Justice of the Supreme Court William Howard Taft, and over 50,000 others in the dedication of the memorial.

It is generally agreed that today the Lincoln Memorial is the most honored and beloved American shrine. Not only is it a testament to the deeds of the great American, but upon its walls are enscribed some of the most eloquent words of mankind and a great nation. From the Gettysburg Address:

" . . . our fathers brought forth on this continent a new nation, conceived in liberty and dedicated to the proposition that all men are created equal."

" . . . that government of the people, by the people, for the people, shall not perish from the earth."

And from Lincoln's Second Inaugural Address:

" . . . with malice toward none, with charity for all, with firmness in the right as God gives us to see the right, let us strive on to finish the work we are in . . ."

On a wall of the monument, the Angel of Truth frees a slave. On another the hands of North and South are joined in a new unity of nation.

Further symbolizing this reunification is the graceful Arlington

Memorial Bridge which connects the Lincoln Memorial with Robert E. Lee's antebellum mansion, the Arlington House, across the Potomac.

But the Lincoln Memorial has come to serve still another historic aspect of American life. Lincoln's freeing of black Americans from the bondage of slavery was given symbolic support on Easter Sunday, 1939. It was then that the great Negro singer, Marian Anderson, was permitted to sing at the memorial after being denied the use of Constitution Hall because of her race.

And on August 28, 1963, Dr. Martin Luther King, Jr., delivered his epic "I Have a Dream" speech before 200,000 Americans. Dr. King pleaded for equal and just treatment of all races.

Today millions of Americans, schoolchildren and adults, along with people from other nations, come annually to the Lincoln Memorial. With deep emotion, they gaze up through the giant pillars at the powerful face of Abraham Lincoln. By it they are inspired to the best of themselves and their country.

They also read in his words the undying hope which the ideal of American democracy offers for all humankind.

JOINING Washington and Lincoln is still another great American president whose achievements have won him an exalted shrine in the nation's capital. Thomas Jefferson's accomplishments were many, but he is most notable to history as the author of the Declaration of Independence. He will forever be remembered for the sacred words of human freedom that unleashed mankind from the bondage of authoritarianism:

"We hold these Truths to be self-evident, that all men are created equal, that they are endowed by their Creator with certain unalienable Rights, that among these are Life, Liberty and the pursuit of Happiness . . . "

In these words of the American Declaration of Independence, Jefferson established the basic premise of a free society. On it rests the entire concept of a democracy. It was, and still is, the essential idea which distinguished the United States of America from the despotic nations of the world.

However, a national shrine in recognition of Jefferson's genius was long in coming. It wasn't until 1938 that the design and location of the memorial were approved. The design chosen for it was a pantheon emulating the temple built by Agrippa at Rome in 27 B.C. From the ancient work, architect John Russell Pope

Below: The Jefferson Memorial, standing on landfill of the Potomac Tidal Basin, is one of Washington's most beautiful shrines.

Right: The majestic nineteen-foot figure of Thomas Jefferson is surrounded by some of the greatest words in the history of mankind.

conceived a pure-white marble temple of simplicity and intense beauty.

Its circular structure is surrounded by an uninterrupted series of majestic Ionic columns which support a domed roof. The dome is similar to that of Jefferson's rotunda at Monticello. The pantheon is fronted with an extended tympanum featuring a continuation of the classic columns.

After much debate, the Jefferson Memorial was located on filled land of the Tidal Basin on a line extending southwesterly from the Capitol down Maryland Avenue. It overlooks the quiet waters of the Basin and the surrounding landscape. Dedicated in 1943, the memorial forms a diamond shape in conjunction with the Capitol, the White House, and the Lincoln Memorial. At the center is the Washington Monument.

Standing inside a central room of the edifice is a nineteen-foot heroic bronze statue. It depicts the trim, erect, intellectually commanding figure of Thomas Jefferson. Cut into the marble wall behind it are the immortal words of the Declaration of Independence.

It is the American credo: *"We hold these truths to be self-evident, that all men are created equal . . ."* With this phrase Jefferson expressed a benevolence and compassion in governance that set a new standard for all the nations of the world.

FROM THE very beginning, American wars have left behind their brave dead heroes. And always those who survive—the families, the friends, and returned comrades, the nation at large—strive to express their sorrowed respect and love for those who perished in the struggle and to honor all the others who served.

The national capital has long been a favored site for memorials commemorating the nation's war dead. The headquarters of the Daughters of the American Revolution (DAR) at Memorial Continental Hall perpetuates the memory of those who helped to achieve American independence. Both it and Constitution Hall house patriotic displays of the Revolutionary War.

The dead of the Civil War, both Northern and Southern, are commemorated by Arlington National Cemetery. The land and the nearby Arlington House estate of Confederate General Robert E. Lee were occupied by Union forces in 1861. Union soldiers camped and drilled beneath its ancient elms and oaks during the Civil War.

In 1864, 210 acres were set aside as a national cemetery for Union soldiers and sailors. The first man buried there was a Confederate soldier. However, he and other Confederate soldiers buried there were later removed. In 1899, a petition by the United Confederate Veterans persuaded President McKinley to permit the reburial of Southern soldiers in Arlington. By this, the cemetery came to signify national reunification.

Today Arlington National Cemetery has been expanded to 612 acres and holds the remains of more than 200,000 veterans and their dependents. A monument to the unknown dead of the Civil War was established in 1866; one to the dead of the Spanish-American War in 1902; to the dead in the *Maine* disaster in 1915. Arlington House is a memorial to Robert E. Lee.

The cemetery is the site of the Tomb of the Unknown Soldier, erected in 1921. The Tomb enshrines the body of a World War I soldier who died in France. Unknown servicemen of World War II, the Korean conflict, and the Vietnam War have since been entombed in front of the crypt.

At Arlington, too, is the Eternal Flame marking the grave of President John F. Kennedy. Just to the north of the cemetery stands the Marine Corps Memorial which depicts U.S. Marines raising the American flag at Iwo Jima during World War II.

The latest Washington war memorial, and certainly one of the most personalized and haunting today, is that commemorating the men and women who died in Vietnam. The Vietnam War was the longest in American history. It involved more than a million

American men and women, over 58,000 of whom were killed or missing and more than 300,000 wounded.

It was also one of America's most controversial wars. The American public was severely split as to participation in it. Pro-war "hawks" felt the United States was obligated to oppose the spread of communism in Asia. Anti-war "doves" believed it was a useless and tragic waste of lives and resources to fight what appeared to be an unwinnable war so far from home.

Vietnam contrasted sharply to World War II when the American public was in strong support of the war effort. Then the American G.I. had returned victoriously in units to great acclaim. But soldiers came back from Vietnam individually, seldom noticed, ill-appreciated, and sometimes scorned. Many of them were maimed—physically as well as psychologically.

The movement to establish a memorial to the American dead of that war was begun by former Vietnam infantryman Jan Scruggs. He was joined by others such as former Air Force officer Robert Doubek and Vietnam veteran John Wheeler in establishing and promoting the Vietnam Veterans Memorial Fund.

With the support of Maryland Senator Charles McC. Mathias, Jr., a bill was pushed through the Congress to erect a memorial on the grounds of the nation's capital. President Jimmy Carter signed it into law in 1980.

There was much debate as to its form. A national competition for a design of the memorial was held. The winning entry was made by a young Yale University art student, Maya Ying Lin. Her design embodied a simple concept. It was a long V-shaped wall of black granite panels, its ends slanting skyward from out of the earth to its apex at the juncture of the two extensions.

The grave of President John F. Kennedy, with its eternal flame, lies at the foot of the hill below the Arlington House and Tomb of the Unknown Soldier in Arlington National Cemetery.

On it, as Scruggs had insisted from the start, would be engraved the name of every man and woman who was lost during the Vietnam War.

The completed memorial was dedicated on Veteran's Day 1982. Situated in the Constitution Gardens of the Mall, one length of the "V" points directly toward the Lincoln Memorial, the other toward the Washington Monument.

Nearby, in stark realism, stands the statue of three servicemen of the Vietnam War. They are young men, decked in their fighting garb and holding their weapons of war. They face toward the long, black wall which carries the names of their comrades who perished in Vietnam.

It is another great memorial of reunification. Americans who come to it—the families, the former comrades, the hawks and the doves—are one again in their common respect and love for those whose names read on like an endless scroll.

Here in justice the Vietnam veteran joins America's heroes of ages past: they who fought and died in the name of America. What better place could they be paid homage than in the nation's capital—George Washington's city of national unity?

Americans find the memories of loved ones, as well as of their own lives, reflected in the somber, name-enscribed walls of the Vietnam Memorial.

Selected Bibliography

Ashabranner, Brent. *Always to Remember*. New York: Dodd, Mead & Company, 1988.

Boyd, Julian P., ed. *The Papers of Thomas Jefferson*. 19 vols. Princeton: Princeton University Press, 1974.

Brooks, Noah. *Washington in Lincoln's Time*. New York: The Century Company, 1895.

Brown, Glenn. *History of the United States Capitol*. 2 vols. Washington: GPO, 1900.

Bryan, Wilhelemus Bryant. *A History of the National Capital from Its Foundation through the Period of the Adoption of the Organic Act*. 2 vols. New York: Macmillan Co., 1914–16.

Caemmerer, H. P. *The Life of Pierre Charles L'Enfant*. Washington: National Republic Publishing Co., 1950.

———. *Washington, the National Capital*. 71st Cong., 3rd sess., *Senate Document 332*. Washington: GPO, 1932.

Carroll, John Alexander. *George Washington*. New York: Charles Scribner's Sons, 1957.

Cresson, W. P. *James Monroe*. Chapel Hill: University of North Carolina Press, 1946.

Development of the United States Capital. Washington: GPO, 1930.

Documentary History of the Construction and Development of the United States Capitol Building and Grounds. 58th Cong., 2d. sess., *House Report 646.* Washington: GPO, 1904.

Federal Writer's Project. *Washington, City and Capital.* Washington: GPO, 1937.

Flexner, James Thomas. *Washington, the Indispensable Man.* Boston: Little Brown & Co., 1969.

Green, Constance McLaughlin. *Washington, Village and Capital, 1800–1878.* Princeton: Princeton University Press, 1962.

Harvey, Frederick L. *History of the Washington National Monument and Washington National Monument Society.* 57th Cong., 2d sess., *Document No. 224.* Washington: GPO, 1903.

Harwell, Richard. *Washington.* As abridged in 2 vols. by Douglas Southall Freeman. New York: Charles Scribner's Sons, 1968.

Hurd, Charles. *The White House Story.* New York: Hawthorne Brothers, Inc., Publishers, 1966.

Jensen, Amy La Follette. *The White House and Its Thirty-two Families.* New York: McGraw Hill Book Co., Inc., 1958.

Kimmel, Stanley. *Mr. Lincoln's Washington.* New York: Coward-McCann, Inc., 1957.

Kite, Elizabeth Sarah. *L'Enfant and Washington, 1791–1792.* Baltimore: Johns Hopkins Press, 1929.

Leish, Kenneth W. *The White House.* New York: Newsweek Book Division, 1972.

Lincoln Memorial. Washington: Department of Interior, 1986.

Lloyd, Allan. *The Scorching of Washington: The War of 1812.* Washington: Robert B. Luce Co., Inc., 1974.

Lord, Walter. *The Dawn's Early Light.* New York: W. W. Norton Co., Inc., 1972.

National Capital Planning Commission. *Worthy of the Nation, the History and Planning for the National Capital.* Washington: Smithsonian Institution Press, 1977.

Padover, Saul K., ed. *The Washington Papers.* New York: Harper Brothers, 1955.

Seale, William. *The President's House*. 2 vols. Washington: White House Historical Society and National Geographic Society and Harry N. Abrams, Inc., 1961.

We the People, the Story of the United States Capitol, Its Past and Its Promise. Washington: U.S. Capitol Historical Society, 1978.

White House Historical Association. *The White House, An Historic Guide*. Washington: National Geographic Society, 1982.

Harper's Weekly

Harper's New Monthly Magazine

National Intelligencer and Washington Advertiser

Washington Evening Star

United States Magazine

Index